THE DEVIL'S FARM

THIS WORLD NOW

RAVEN GULLEY

OTHER BOOKS BY RAVEN GULLEY

REAPERS WINGS
OUTLAWS AWAKENED
RIDING INTO FIRE
A BLOODY GOODBYE

IT'S BEEN three months since the world ended. Three months that have been nothing but hell and back for most people. Most people haven't learned to live without having electricity and running water. They had grown into their luxuries they had every day. Luxuries that are no longer here anymore.

These three months haven't been hell and back for me. It's opened up my eyes to a lot of things. I took a lot of things for granted, like ordinary people. I can overcome this world we're living in now. As an army veteran who served this United States for twenty years, I've come face-to-face with hard times in battle.

A war has developed against mankind so that we can salvage what's left of food and toiletries. The national guard has moved into town. They are rationing everything between families. I don't know how much longer we will be able to sustain it before it gets out of control. For now everything's okay, but I suspect that will change.

It started off as a deadly virus. One of those viruses where you have aches and chills. The one where you sleep your day away because you're too sick to do anything else. When people started waking up from this virus, they didn't wake up as people. They woke up as something else.

I've never seen anything like it. Watching these zombies rip into other people's flesh and devour them like food. Those people who have become victims of zombies turn into these things too. We've always got to watch our backs. Because if we get bitten, we'll turn into a zombie. It's like taking a journey into hell. Except that's what life is like now. Living is hell. Since life belongs to the devil himself.

I pull up my jeans and grab my bag full of dirty laundry. Now it's time for my son Landon and I to go get our box of supplies. I'm clean since I bathed in the river. It's the best thing about living here in the boonies. There's always going to be a water supply.

He turns around and looks down at me. He's on the top of the hill, watching for zombies. None have ventured out this way yet. "You ready to go, old man?"

I don't know who the hell he's calling old man. Forty isn't old in my book and hasn't ever been. "When we get back, the two of us need to plow the garden."

He nods. "It's too hot out right now. We can get it done when the sun goes down."

I walk up the hill and join him. "The last thing we need is to have a heat stroke."

He takes the bag out of my hands and puts it in the garage. I'll rinse them out and hang them up when we get back. "I hope we'll get something good in our box this week."

I personally don't care what we get in our box. I'll eat anything if it keeps me from going hungry. My son isn't like me. He's a twenty-year-old kid who hasn't truly endured hardships yet.

"I'm hoping we'll get some canned food," I say before getting into the car.

Canned food will last us for a week, maybe two.

He slides into the passenger seat. "Maybe we'll see old Henry today."

Henry used to be a preacher at the church we went to. He's my definition of an old man since he's in his eighties.

"I'm sure his daughters are taking good care of him."

Henry doesn't live alone. His family—other than his wife, who died a year ago—are still alive the last I heard.

I start the car, and I pull into our dirt driveway. To a lot of people, it might be scary having the river on the other side of you, without guardrail. But I'm familiar with driving these curvy roads.

He nods. "You're probably right."

I'm not a big fan of hip hop, but I turn up one of Landon's old cds. There's no radio station, and it's better than sitting here in silence.

He peers out the window, looking at the beauty of the mountains, I assume. "Do you think we're going to stay the rest of our lives at the farm?" he asks.

I turn down the music and grip the steering wheel. "I hope we can, but I don't know."

Landon doesn't reply back, but bites down on his lip and wrinkles his brow. It makes me wonder what he's thinking about.

I don't want to think about leaving the farm. It's our safe haven and our home. The place we've been for the last year. There's no need to walk away from it right now. Hopefully we'll never have to. Either way, it's not anything to dwell on. For now, it's our home and the only thing that matters.

The disgusting pieces of decaying flesh, aka the zombies, are on the side of the road when we get two miles away from town. I wish I could take my gun and blow their brains out. If I had a lot of bullets, I would, but it would be something stupid to do now.

I go past the swimming pool, and my eye catches on a

petite figure walking around the track. Her shorts are cut just at the middle of her thighs, and she walks tall, an indication she isn't one of them. A car is parked close by. I speed up, not wanting Landon to see her. He wants to save everyone we come across, but not everyone can be saved. Sometimes you just have to keep moving.

"Do you think things will ever go back to what they used to be?" He swivels away from the window, and his gaze lands on me.

I divert my gaze from the road for a brief second. "You're asking me something I don't know." I quickly focus back on the road. "There might be a place that's more developed with electricity and running water. I can't even begin to imagine where a place like that would be though."

He squeezes my shoulder. "Thanks for being honest with me, old man."

"I wouldn't dare bullshit you."

"That's what makes you a hard ass."

I've never heard those words come out of his mouth before.

I laugh. "I guess that's one way of looking at things."

When we reach the old grocery store, there's several other vehicles in the parking lot. A man who's got a ball cap on his head smirks at me. He's got a gun in his hands.

This isn't what I was expecting. The national guard was just here last week.

I crack my knuckles and roll my neck to the side. "Stay here and don't move. I'm going to see what his fucking deal is."

He rubs his pant legs. "I don't like the looks of this."

I don't either but I'm going to try to keep the peace. "Believe me when I say everything's going to be alright."

He nods but there's uncertainty on his face. "Things have got to be okay."

I open up the door to the car and put my hand on the gun at my hip. It's something that will always give me comfort. "My name's Joey and my son Landon is with me. We've just come here to get food. We don't mean you any harm."

The man takes a step closer to me. "I hate to break it to you but this grocery store doesn't belong to you. It belongs to me and my people. I would suggest you get in your car and leave."

I ball up my fists at my side. "There's nowhere else to go in this county. Please don't make us leave. We're just asking for anything you have to spare."

The man's eyes are ice cold when he gets out his gun. "I'm not telling you again, get in your car. This isn't something up for debate."

A flash of red flashes before my eyes. I'm not leaving until I have a few choice words with him. I can't be certain he's even going to use that gun. "You think that I'm scared of you? I could take you down in a heartbeat."

A bullet lands at my feet and a woman appears from on top of the rooftop. "He might be afraid to end you but I'm sure as hell not. If you're not gone in the next couple of minutes, you'll be dead."

You no good pieces of shit are going to get everything coming to you.

I stroll back to the car and open up the door. "Looks like this place isn't one we can go to anymore."

He shakes his head in disgust. "You did the right thing by walking away."

I'm not so sure about that. If he wouldn't have been with me I would have taken them both down. I wouldn't have thought twice about it.

I start the engine and pull out of the parking lot as another vehicle pulls in. "This is just the start of all the bad things that are going to happen."

He wrinkles his nose. "Where are we going now, old man?"

It couldn't be any more obvious he doesn't want to talk about the hell we're about to endure.

"To the city to get Heather and Brooke."

I PEEK out the window and spot zombies stumbling on the side of the street. Now's the time to do what I came here to do. I can't stay here another couple of hours and risk it getting dark out. This hospital's too big for me to be in it all alone.

"Please just let me go," Damon pleads with me.

This isn't the first time he's pled for his life today. He should know by now he's not getting out of this alive.

His legs are strapped down to the hospital bed, making it impossible for him to move. I'm not going to give this guy any sympathy. Fuck sympathy. He didn't have an ounce of it when his drunk ass got behind the wheel and killed my little boy.

I get my boy's picture out of my wallet and hold it up for him to see. "Do you remember him?" I demand.

Damon blinks his eyes. "I can't say that I've ever seen him before."

I put the picture back in my wallet and stick it into my pocket.

Rage ignites inside of me, hot tendrils of fury spreading through my veins. "That's my boy you fucking killed! You think I'm doing this for fun?"

Damon's face twists in pain. "I remember that little boy

now. I'm so sorry for what I've done. If you let me out of here, I'll do whatever you ask."

He's not getting out of this fucking hospital. I drove four hours to get here. I'm not just going to let him get away.

I get the gun out of my pants and point it at his head. The tendons stand out in his neck, and beads of sweat drip down his face. There's no satisfaction until he's no longer breathing. "You're not doing anything except staying here while I blow your fucking head off!"

Screams erupt from his lips. "Please, someone help me!"

There's no one around. I made sure of that four days ago. I wanted to keep this fucker to myself so I could torture him and do what the fuck I want. It's the right thing to do. The only thing that has consumed my mind these past couple of days.

I put my finger on the trigger, ready to pull it any time. "Nobody's here. I would suggest you shut the fuck up."

Tears stream down his face. "I understand why you're doing this. I really do. You seem like a good guy, and this will eat away at your soul."

He doesn't know anything about me. So how can he say this is going to eat away at my soul?

I'm done talking to him. He's trying to stall me and I don't have any time to waste.

The sound of ferocious growls echoes through the air. A shudder runs up and down my spine. These fucking zombies are in here, and I don't know how many of them there are.

I put my gun back into my pants. "Say hello to the devil when you join him in hell. Let him know I'll be coming there next."

He raises up, and his mouth falls open. "You can't just leave me here for those things."

I open up the window, prepared to get the fuck out of here. "I can, and I will."

The door opens, and what used to be a woman comes into

the room. Her hair's red, and she's missing an arm. Snarls escape from her lips, and she makes her way towards Damon. I watch her sink her teeth into him. Blood squirts in every direction, and screams pour past his lips. It's probably going to take her a while to finish him off. As much as I want to, I can't stand around for that.

A zombie blocks my path to my truck. I shoot it in the head, and it goes down.

I run past it and hop into the driver's side. I start the engine and prepare to get out of here. Happiness runs through my body, having seen that fucker in pain. It's a more suitable death for him being ripped apart by zombies. Heat radiates through my chest since he's in more pain than he would've been if I shot him.

My lips press together in a grimace, and a lump forms in my throat. While I'm happy the fucker is going to be dead soon, it's a shame the numbness my heart still has. Killing him didn't bring my boy back.

I strum my fingers on the steering wheel. Now's the time to figure out where to go next. I'm not staying in this city tonight. It's like a death sentence waiting to happen.

I think back to the river me and my boy used to fish at. It's away from the city and in a small town. I'll be able to get there before nightfall.

My little boy's wrangled body comes to mind. I shove the image out of my head. I've got to focus on surviving. He's something I can't think about. There's always time to have a breakdown later. Now, to get to the house in one piece before night comes. It should be an easy task but is probably going to be a difficult one.

CHAPTER 3
AVA

THE SOUND of a gunshot from outside vibrates through the house, and my stomach twists in knots. I go to the window and stare at a man who's wearing a prison jumpsuit. A body of a woman lies in the grass by his feet.

I've got to get out of here before he comes in here for me. The back door to my house opens, and I freeze. Oh God, he's got an accomplice, and I didn't get to lock the door in time. I'm dead as dead can be.

Angel peeks his head into the living room, and relief washes over me. He's been my best friend ever since high school. Even though that was twenty years ago. "I'm glad I got here in time. There's a group of them. We've got to go now, before we become their next victims."

A wave of sadness washes over me. This is my home, and to leave it because of these disgusting human beings is beyond me. I don't have anywhere else to go. My grandmother, the woman who raised me, passed away last year. She's the only family I had.

I follow behind him as we step outside into the hot summer air. There isn't another man in sight. If they're in groups, I'm sure they can't be far.

Angel ducks behind a bush and motions for me to join him. "We've got to make a run across the street to my car."

Fear eats me alive at the thought of crossing the street. Not only have we got zombies to look out for, but monstrous human beings. I clear my throat. "How many more of them are out here?"

Sweat drips from Angel's forehead. "I don't know. I've only seen five of them."

I grip the cross necklace around my neck. "Okay. Let's do this."

Angel squeezes my hand. "Keep running, and don't look back."

My body trembles at the very thought of being out in the open. This is the first time I've set foot outside my house in the last week. I didn't think I would have to leave like this.

I take a deep breath and start running. The wind blows my blonde hair across my face, and I push it away. The area's completely empty except for his car. Maybe these disgusting human beings are somewhere else. I hope and pray they don't come around any time soon.

The man in the jumpsuit peeks his head from the corner of my house. I kneel down on the ground so he doesn't see me. I wish he would just leave so Angel's cover wouldn't be blown.

Crippling fear cuts into Angel's eyes, widening them and making the familiar brown turn almost black. My entire body aches for him to be near me. He's got to come out of this alive. I don't know what I'm going to do without him.

The man in the jumpsuit steps onto my front porch. "This is the nicest house on the block. It's going to be a perfect place to set up."

Anger runs through my body. The house he's talking about is mine. It has been mine for the past ten years. Fucking bastard. He's got no right to take it away from me. Not after I've worked so hard for it.

The guy in the jumpsuit steps inside my house. I lick my lips, and my heart batters fast against my chest.

Come on, Angel, while you still can!

I take a deep breath when Angel runs towards me. My stomach churns, and his pace escalates. His long legs make quick strides, and he comes to me unannounced. That could have ended badly.

When we both get into the car, I give him a hug. "I wouldn't be alive if it wasn't for you," I say.

He starts the car engine. "We're not at the farm yet."

"Where's this farm you're talking about?" I ask.

Angel pulls out of the parking lot. "Do you remember my grandmother's house?"

How could I forget it? Lots of good memories were made at that house. We would have parties there as teenagers and go fishing in the river. That place was where I spent the majority of my teenage years. Then when my twenties hit, I quit going there. I had to since his grandparents both died in a car accident. A short time after that, his parents sold the place.

"I remember that place like the back of my hand." Curiosity gets the best of me. "What has made you decide that you want to go there?"

I don't think he's been back there since then. For all we know, it could be in ruins. There might not even be a house withstanding. I push those thoughts out of my mind. We've got to have a roof over our head. It's our biggest chance of survival.

"A few months back, I got curious about what's happened to the place. So I went to look around. It looks even better than what I envisioned it to be. Whoever bought it tore down my grandparents' old home and built a new one."

A house being there is comforting. Now let's just hope whoever is living there isn't a psychopath. I'm leaning on faith since that's all I've got.

Cars are lined up on the road in front of us. At this rate, we'll be sitting here for the next hour.

Angel's lips turn down in a frown. He pulls the car over to the side of the road. "I've got two knives, and a baseball bat. Our best option is to walk until we get closer to town."

Is he out of his fucking mind? This is crazy. The best option isn't walking. It's waiting this shit out. The undead are out there and people who just tried to kill us. How are we going to stay protected out in the open?

I stammer on my words. "Angel, I don't think that walking is such a good idea."

He turns off the car and leans over to give me a hug. "I'm going to be with you every step of the way. I don't plan on leaving you, Ava. The two of us are in this together."

He's your best friend. This is your best chance at survival. This car could've broken down before you started going again.

I squeeze his hand and take a deep breath. "Okay. Let's go."

He hands me one of the knives and puts the other knife in his pocket. "There's an old woman I know a couple of blocks away. She's got a car full of gas. It's just a matter of persuading her to leave."

Okay. That's not too bad.

I'm more than ready to do this.

I open up the door to the car before I lose my courage. "You can lead the way."

I GO the long way around to avoid the cars on the interstate. It's been a smooth journey down here, and I'm amazed. We've seen zombies on the side of the road. There's been more of them the closer we get to the city. People are a different story. We've not seen a single soul.

Landon rubs his pant legs. "I sure hope we didn't come all this way for nothing."

I'm almost certain Brooke and Heather have not gone anywhere. Brooke won't let Heather leave since she's waiting for her boyfriend, Matt. Matt lived in South Carolina before this apocalypse hit. There's no telling where he is. For all we know, he could be dead.

Anger erupts inside me thinking about what happened at the grocery store. "If nothing else, we've got to go searching for food. It wouldn't be a wise idea to go back home empty-handed."

I pull into the parking lot of Heather's apartment. Four zombies are banging on her door, begging to be let inside.

His eyes go wide. "Are you seeing this right now?"

I turn off the car and glance over at him. "I see it alright, and that's why you need to stand behind me."

He nods. "You don't have to tell me twice."

Fury ignites the inferno burning inside me. I hate these fucking zombies. They're the reason why the world's like it is. The hell's just beginning, and it's the shitty thing about it.

I take out my gun as the two of us make our way up the stairs. One of the zombies looks at me. The red eyes send chills up and down my spine. They're demonic creatures created by the devil himself.

I shoot them all in the head, and they fall to the ground since their brains are no more. I take a deep breath as panic sets in. I haven't been back here in a week. Surely nothing has happened to Heather or Brooke.

Landon's hand shakes on my shirt. "I need to get used to fighting these things."

I turn around and stare into his frightened green eyes. "I'll teach you to fight these things when we get back home."

He gives me an understanding nod. "Let's see if they're here, old man."

I open the door to the house and brace myself for what's inside. The couch and table are both turned over. Knots form in my stomach as I think the worst has happened. "Brooke! Heather! Are you two here?" I call.

"We're both in the closet!" Heather yells back.

Relief washes over me. "Get your things so we can leave!"

I hold my gun out in front of me, and the bedroom door flies open. Heather's face is two shades paler, and she licks her lips. "We've been in there ever since this morning," she says.

Brooke comes out the door behind Heather. "How can you make us leave? Matt expects me to be here."

I'm not surprised to hear this coming from Brooke. "Get your stuff so we can get out of here. We've got to make a pit stop in town to get food."

Brooke stares at me like I've said something foreign. "Did you not listen to what I just said?"

I refuse to stand here and do this with her. "I'm not going

to tell you again. Get your shit. We have to get out of here now."

Heather touches Brooke's arm. "Do what he says, baby."

Brooke slams the door shut to the bedroom. "I don't know how you could ever side with him!"

Heather's got a carry-on bag on her back. "Some man came here a couple of hours ago. He scared the hell out of me. The only thing I knew to do was hide from him. Thank God you showed up when you did."

Landon goes to the window. "Dad, we've got to get going. There's a horde of undead coming our way."

I stare out the window to see what he's talking about. A couple of yards away, the undead are coming towards us. Their heads are tilted on their necks, and they have a slow, steady walk about them. In just a matter of minutes, they'll be at the car. "Brooke, for fuck's sake, grab your things so we can go."

Brooke storms out of the bedroom. "I'm here. Are you happy now?"

I clench my fists and try to keep my cool. Brooke's always been a brat, and it hasn't changed now. "I'll be happy when we get back home, and all of us are in one piece."

Landon steps away from the window. "Dad, we've got to go now."

I step outside the apartment with Brooke, Landon, and Heather trailing behind me. I'm going to teach every single one of them how to fight. There might come a time when I won't be here. They're going to have to survive on their own. "Listen to me. Everyone needs to make a run for the car."

Landon does the counting. "One, two, three."

We take off running, and Brooke stumbles on the pavement. Tears stream down her face, and I grab ahold of her hand. "Just leave me here. Life isn't worth living without Matt," Brooke says.

I roll my eyes and put my gun away. This is complete and

utter bullshit. I scoop her up like a baby and carry her to the car. A zombie's gaining on us and will be here within seconds. Brooke screams, and I wish she would shut the hell up. Her screams are going to draw more attention to us.

Landon shoots the zombie, and it hits the shoulder. "Dad, come on." His voice is filled with urgency.

It's not every day I carry a one hundred twenty-pound woman. I'm going as fast as I can.

Landon fires the gun again. This time he doesn't miss.

I set Brooke down, and she gets into the car, slamming the door behind her.

This was quite an adventure. Now I don't have any reason to come back to the city.

I slide myself into the car, out of harm's way, and take several deep breaths. "Don't you ever stop fighting, Brooke. You're young and have your entire life ahead."

Heather leans across the seat and gives me a hug. It catches me off guard, and I remind myself she's off-limits. The two of us are divorced for a reason. "Thank you for everything. We wouldn't have survived much longer if it wasn't for you," Heather says.

I start the engine and pull out of the parking lot. "You're more capable than what you think you are."

Heather's lip trembles. "I don't have a gun or many weapons. The only things I have are a knife and a pair of scissors. My car needs gas, so you're wrong about that. We were shit out of luck before you came along."

Nothing is funny, but I laugh anyway. She never was big on filling up her car. It's something I would always do. "How are you doing back there, Landon? Brooke?"

Brooke glares at me. "I fucking hate you for making me leave."

This isn't the first time I'm the bad guy. Let's just say I was a horrible husband who treated Heather like shit. I would hook up with other women and stay out all weekend drunk.

Brooke has never liked me ever since then. I can't say I blame her.

I challenge her by glancing at her through the rearview mirror. "Leaving was the only option. The two of you couldn't stay in that closet forever."

Landon's stomach growls. "I don't want to sound like a nuisance, but I'm starving."

"Are there any places that we can get food?" I ask.

Heather strums her thumbs against the dashboard. "Let's try that old grocery store fifteen minutes away. There's bound to be something there."

Sobs escape from Brooke's lips. "You were a horrible excuse for a man. I'm sure you're still nothing but a fucking drunk."

I don't say anything since there's nothing left to say. It's going to be a long car ride back.

I STUMBLE through the woods and struggle to catch my breath. Angel's long legs are a struggle to keep up with. He's six foot and is a couple of inches taller than me. "You've got to slow down," I say.

Angel keeps pushing through the overgrown brush. "We don't have time to stop. We'll be there in less than ten minutes."

A zombie peeks out from around the corner. The shirt the zombie's wearing is ripped to shreds, and an arm is barely hanging onto the bone. My eyes go wide since this isn't a nightmare I can escape from. "Angel, there's a zombie heading our way," I say.

He grips my shirt. "Come on. Who knows how many more of them are coming."

I follow Angel as we make our way farther into the woods. Trees and bushes are the only things that surround us. Sweat drips off my forehead. It's got to be at least ninety degrees out. I would love to have a water right now. My throat's parched from the heat. "I'm not going to make it," I reply.

I'm physically fit but not used to this shit. I used to walk my ass off at the gym on a treadmill. A place that was air conditioned. Now the sun's rays are eating me alive. There's not any part of my body that's not soaking wet.

He shakes his head. "You're doing just fine. You've got this."

It's just the reassurance I need to keep moving forward.

A decaying hand wraps around my foot, and I scream. The undead makes its appearance known by coming out of the bush. Without thinking twice about it, I take the knife and plunge it into its head. Now isn't the time to quit. It's time to hurry along.

I shudder. That was too close for comfort.

He leans forward to examine the back of my thigh. "It didn't bite you, did it?" His voice deepens.

No, it didn't bite me. Thank God it didn't. It was a close call, and now I'm ready to get out of these woods.

I shake my head. "Let's keep going. You said something about only having a couple minutes left."

He lets go of me, and we push on.

There's a house up ahead of us. It's so close and within our grasp.

Just keep pushing a little farther. You're almost there.

A grin forms on my face. We're so close to being out of the sun and on our way to the farm.

His brown eyes sparkle, and the muscles in his cheekbones relax. "I knew you could do it."

I step out of the woods and into the driveway. "I couldn't have done any of this without you."

He stops walking to gaze into my eyes. "You would have been just fine on your own."

I'm not so sure about that. All I can think about is what would have happened if he wasn't here. I would go crazy without him. He's the only person I've talked to these past three months. The two of us have been staying together in my house.

The only time we've had to leave was to get supplies. We

would come to the store and get whatever we could find. We've not been apart since this apocalypse happened. I don't want to ever think about being apart.

He opens the door to the house. My body shakes, and the hair stands up on my arms.

Please don't let anything happen, God. Just let us get this old lady, her car, and leave.

I clutch my arms against my chest, the chills running up and down my spine.

"Daisy, are you here?" Angel calls.

I glance around the kitchen that consists of a table, chairs, refrigerator, and freezer. Just everything you would find in one. My heart beats fast against my chest. I wonder if anyone's here.

Relax. Everything's fine.

I walk towards Angel, who's now made his way into the living room. "I don't think anyone's here," I say.

Footsteps from a nearby bedroom proves otherwise.

I don't understand if someone's here, why they won't say anything. Not unless they are a bad person or human being. Anybody who's good would speak unless they have something to be afraid of.

I touch Angel's arm. "Be careful. We don't know what's here."

He clears his throat. "Daisy wouldn't have left. She's got to be here."

An uneasiness forms over me, and my chest tightens. "If she's here, she would have said something."

He ignores my comment and puts his hand on the door handle. "We'll be out of here in the next couple of minutes."

A woman with white hair lunges at Angel. Her teeth clamp down onto the flesh of his arm. My heart sinks since he's not going to make it out of this alive.

Angel screams out in pain, and I jab the knife into the

woman's skull. She loosens her grip on him and falls to the floor.

I go to Angel, the tears streaming down my face. This is the end of our adventure. Now I'm not going to have anyone else left in this world.

He puts his head in my lap and winces in pain. "Daisy's keys should be in her car. You get the hell out of here and don't look back."

Sobs escape from my chest, and a waterfall escapes from my eyes. "I'm not ready to leave you yet. I can't go."

He gasps for air. "I could turn at any time. Get the hell out of here."

You've got to let him go. Even though it hurts.

I lay him down on the floor, still not ready to depart without him yet. This is the last time I'll ever see him. There's no pictures of him with me except for all of the memories inside my head. "I'm staying right here with you until you turn."

His body trembles, and sweat drips off his face. "Promise me something."

"What is it?" I choke out the words.

"Promise me you'll go to this farm and find happiness."

"Of course I will."

His body goes still, and he closes his eyes.

You need to do it now. Goodbye, Angel.

I take the knife out of my pocket and plunge it into Angel's head. Blood cakes onto the knife, and I wipe it on my shirt. He's really gone and not coming back.

My chest is heavy, and my body goes completely numb. The one person who I thought was going to be around a long time is gone. We're never going to have any more conversations together or make memories. Today will forever be the worst day of my life.

THE UNDEAD SURROUND the grocery store, and I refuse to stop. It would be like a death sentence waiting to happen, and I'm not willing to risk it. There's got to be a place somewhere else we can go on the way back. We just need to keep our eyes open.

"I'm sorry. I thought this was a good place to go," Heather says.

"You don't have anything to be sorry about," I reply.

I'm sure she hasn't been out of the house much.

Brooke's eyes are closed. Which is probably the reason she's not said anything in the last couple of minutes. How she could sleep at a time like this, I don't know.

Passing by all of these abandoned businesses is like looking at a ghost town. The businesses that were once opened are now abandoned. Windows are blown out of several of them. Several of the undead are walking along the street. You would think they are human beings. They look like ordinary people, but what distinguishes them as the undead is their red eyes. One of them parts their lips, and the teeth are still intact.

Cars are lined up going both ways, and the sign we pass at the gas station is upside down. There is a herd of twenty undead. They line the sidewalk, searching for their next meal. "We don't have to stop to get anything," Landon starts to say.

"We're stopping when we get closer to the farm," I answer.

This will be the last time we get the car out for a while. It just makes sense to search for food. We don't have the gas to waste, and it might not be as it is now when we come back out.

"I never did thank you for coming to get the two of us." Heather's voice cracks.

"You don't have to thank me. It was just a matter of time before I came to get you," I answer.

Heather gives my arm a friendly squeeze. "There's something I have been wanting to talk to you about. Now seems like the perfect time, while we're both still alive. It's something I didn't tell you back then."

I'm not entirely sure where this is going. I don't want to go talking about the way things were. All of that is in the past and not something that can be changed. We're living in the present now.

"Go ahead," I say, urging her to continue.

If she has something to tell me, it's best for her to let it out. To me it doesn't matter about Landon being in the backseat. There's no reason to keep this from him.

Heather clears her throat. "I had a one-night stand before you started cheating on me."

"I know you did." I laugh. "It's the reason I started cheating on you in the first place."

One of my buddies had seen her kissing another guy at a hotel. He told me, and I didn't confront her about it. I just cheated on her back. It was immature and stupid, but she had hurt me.

Heather shifts in her seat and stares out the window. "Do you think we could've worked things out?"

I think about what I'm going to say. I don't want to come

across as an asshole. "The two of us were young and wild. We had a lot of growing up to do. At the end of the day, I don't think so."

"I hope the two of you didn't get married just because of me," Landon chimes in from the back seat.

I hope my son knows me better than that. I would never marry a woman I didn't love. And I did love Heather. More than anyone since. "You were just an extra sweet package to the deal," Heather says.

I squint my eyes, and I'll be damned if it's our lucky day. There's no undead in the parking lot up ahead and no threat of other people. It's completely empty except for a couple of parked cars. I'm willing to take the chance of going here. We'll get in and get out in record time.

I drum my feet against the floor, and a lightness forms in my chest. An entire load has lifted off my shoulders. Hopefully this place will have the supplies we need.

Brooke rubs her eyes. "Please tell me we're almost there."

I give my signal and then turn into the parking lot.

Heather turns around in her seat to pat Brooke's leg. "We're not quite there, baby. Just a little while longer."

I roll my eyes. It's no surprise Brooke's a brat. Heather treats her like a child when she's a young woman who's eighteen. "You ladies need to stay here and watch the car. Me and Landon are going inside to see what we can find."

Fear flashes in Landon's eyes. "I guess I can go in there with you," he says with uncertainty in his voice.

I open the door to the car. "You're going to be just fine. I will be right there beside you."

Landon looks at me with uncertainty. He gets the gun out of his pants. "Alright. I'm ready to do this, old man."

I pat his shoulder. "Have confidence. This makes you a brave son of a bitch."

Landon cracks a smile. "I will never be as brave as you, old man. You'll always be my hero."

His words touch my soul. If he only knew how much I love him.

The two of us begin to walk up to the grocery store doors. I tilt my head to the side and get my gun out. "Stay focused on what we're about to do."

Landon clears his throat. "What's the game plan?"

My heart hammers out of my chest. We've got to be ready and not let our guards down. "We're going to grab a buggy when we get in the door and load it up."

Landon nods at me uneasily. "I never did think the world would go to shit in my lifetime."

I stifle a grin at his humor. "I didn't think it would either."

Please don't let anything happen to my son. I'm begging you, God. I can't bear to even think about living without him.

I put my hand on the door, and it opens. I scan the area all around me and try to draw in my surroundings. Candy is scattered across the floor. Shelves have been flipped over. There doesn't appear to be any humans or undead here. One thing I can't be is uncertain.

Landon is two steps ahead of me. He grabs a buggy, and the two of us make our way to the canned food section. "I hope we're able to get a lot of food."

There are a few cans of green beans, potatoes, and carrots on the shelves. Landon and I quickly put them in the buggy.

Footsteps walk across the tile, and I search all around me, trying to find the direction they're coming from. "My name's Joey, and I'm with my son, Landon. We just came here to get supplies. We'll soon be on our way."

Landon's lip trembles, and the tendons in his neck stand out. "Dad, we should just go. This should last for a couple of days."

We don't need it to last a couple of days. It needs to last a couple of weeks. I don't want to come back out here searching for supplies.

The footsteps come closer, and I put my finger across my lips. "Whoever's in here is alive," I whisper.

"How do you know that?" Landon asks.

"They're not scuffling their feet," I respond.

I cock my gun, ready to shoot whoever's in here with us. Things would be different if they would've just let themselves be known. It would have been the right thing to do.

A man appears before the two of us. He bites down on his lip and puts his hands out in front of him. His short brown hair is disheveled on his head. "I don't mean to do you two any harm. I've been here a couple of days. The two of you startled me."

I keep my gun trained on him. "Why the hell didn't you say anything when I called out?"

The man shakes his head. "I don't know, man. Just cut me a break."

Landon grabs ahold of my shirt. "There's no need for you to have the gun out. Just let him go. He didn't try anything on us when we walked through the door."

I'm not so sure if I trust him. He's someone I'm not acquainted with.

"Landon, fill up the rest of the buggy so we can get the hell out of here," I demand.

Landon does as I say.

The man's clothes are ragged with holes in them. He's got a distinct body odor that will knock a person off their feet. Maybe what he says is the truth. Even if it is, I can't let my guard down.

"My name's Timmy, and you can put that thing down," he says.

He doesn't tell me what to fucking do. Hell, nobody does.

I don't know who he is or what his intentions are. He didn't say anything when we first walked in the door. He's fucking crazy if he thinks I'm putting my gun down.

I keep the gun trained on him. "Out of all the places you could be, why are you here?"

Timmy stutters on his words. "Some people are after me, and this is where I escaped to."

I take a step back and gape at him. "There's got to be a reason for that," I say, wanting to know more.

Landon puts the rest of the canned food in the buggy.

Screams from outside make my body tingle. I roll my shoulders and then go to the window. Brooke and Heather are outside of the car. Someone I don't recognize is in the driver's side.

You're not getting away with this, mother fucker. We need this car to get back to the farm!

I run out the door without thinking twice about it. I'm not fast enough. The car hightails it out of the parking lot and disappears out of sight.

This day just got a hell of a lot worse. I pace around the parking lot. I'm so angry. I can't fucking see straight. "Why would you let them take the car?" I demand.

Landon steps outside with the buggy. "What happened to the car?"

Heather's eyes fill with rage. "They had guns in their hands! What did you expect us to do!"

Brooke drops her head down. "I unlocked my door for them. If you're blaming anyone, you should be blaming me."

Timmy joins us. "I'd be more than happy for you folks to stay with me."

Timmy must be out of his fucking mind. People are looking for him, which means it's not safe for us to stay here.

"That's not going to happen," I snap.

Brooke strolls away from all of us. "I'm not going to stand here another minute listening to you. You should have never come and got us!"

Landon stares after her. "What are we going to do now?"

Now we're stuck out here in the city because of the two of

them. I can't help but lose my cool. "I don't know what we're going to fucking do! Maybe you should ask Heather and Brooke why they let people take the car. They're the ones who got us in this mess."

Heather shakes her head in disgust. "That's not fair, and you know it isn't. I remember why I divorced you now."

I sink to the ground and try to get ahold of my emotions. A beer would be nice right about now. I'm tempted to go back inside and open up a bottle.

Landon pats my back, and it gives me comfort. "We're going to be alright. Just get ahold of yourself. Think about what we should do next."

I didn't mean to snap at him. It's good to know he's not mad at me. My relationship with him is the only thing that matters. "We need to find a car. If we don't, there's no way in hell we'll make it to the farm by nightfall."

CHAPTER 7
SUNNY

A MAN'S sitting on the ground in the parking lot. There's a couple of people around him. The undead are coming up the sidewalk and will be in the parking lot where they are in the next couple of minutes. It doesn't seem like something they're worried about.

I shouldn't care. I should just keep on driving. But I can't allow myself to be consumed with thoughts of my boy. If I do, it will rip my heart in two. It will be nice having these folks to talk to. It's better than being alone any day.

I pull my truck over to where the guy's now standing. His back is turned to me, and he turns around to look at me. My eyes land on his jaw that's set in a tight line and green eyes I couldn't ever forget. My mouth falls open, and I do a double take. I know these people and have for a hell of a long time. Joey and I were in the army together. It's a damn good thing I'm here now. I'm saving his ass.

I roll down my window. "All of you look like you could use a ride. Hop in."

Joey grins as soon as he realizes it's me. "I thought we were fucked."

I shake my head. "Not on my watch. So get the hell in so we can get going."

Joey takes a step back to help Landon put the canned food in the truck. "Everybody needs to get in the truck now."

I recognize Heather with her long black hair and slender figure. Brooke is the spitting image of her, just a younger version. The only difference being Heather has blue eyes, and Brooke has brown. The two of them hop into the backseat.

I look through the rearview mirror at the zombies headed our way. "Joey, you and Landon better get your ass in this truck."

I'm not about to waste any of my bullets. I don't have any more on me other than the rounds in the chamber. Used them all coming here since there were a lot of fucking zombies on the highway.

Landon folds his arms across his chest. "I'm not going anywhere without Timmy."

I roll my eyes. Landon's always been such a good-hearted person. That's probably not something that will ever change. He cares a little too much about people and always has.

Joey clenches his teeth and balls up his fists at his side. "Alright. There's no room for him with us. He's going in the back."

Timmy hops into the back of the truck. "I could never repay all of you for this."

Joey's green eyes are cold. "You better not do anything to make me regret this."

Landon gets into the truck next to Heather. It's going to be a tight squeeze with his long legs, but they'll manage. "I'm sorry, guys," Landon says.

Brooke lets out a grin. "I can't believe this. I have no leg room."

Could be worse. Zombies could be devouring you right now. So shut the fuck up.

I press my lips together, and the muscles in my neck tense up. I'd like to say a couple choice words to her. She should appreciate my hospitality. I hold my tongue since I don't want to get shit started.

Joey hops into the passenger seat and slams the door shut behind him. "What are you doing in these parts?"

The last time the two of us talked was last summer. It's been a year and seems like a hell of a long time ago. I had come up to see him with my little boy. We stayed an entire week and had the time of our lives. Most of our time had been spent fishing and jumping on the trampoline. A lump forms in my throat, thinking about my little boy. I push those thoughts out of my mind.

"I had some business I needed to take care of," I say.

There's no way in hell I'll tell him about everything that's happened. Not with everyone else around. They'll end up thinking I'm some sort of psycho or something. I did what I had to, and I'll never regret it.

Joey leans forward and strums his fingers across the dashboard. "Where are you headed?"

It's funny for him to ask that question. "To your farm. I was hoping you would still be there."

Joey laughs. "Guess me and Landon are going to have some company."

Damn right you are. I'm not leaving for nothing. It's the perfect place to be away from everyone and everything.

Curiosity gets the best of me. "What's with the guy in the truck bed?"

I'm certain the guy isn't with Joey, judging by the way things were.

Joey shakes his head. "Nothing is with him. When we get back to the farm, we're going to watch him like a hawk. Just to make sure he doesn't try anything."

Landon lets out a sigh in frustration. "If I thought he was going to try anything, I wouldn't have wanted to bring him."

He's just a kid who doesn't have a good sense of judgment.

Joey rubs the back of his neck but ignores the comment. "It looks like we're going to have to turn back around and go the long way."

Cars are lined up on the road in front of us. A man up ahead has a bat in his hand and is surrounded by the undead. There are five of them gathered around him. He swings the bat and hits one in what used to be a stomach. Another one bites down on his arm, ripping off the flesh. Blood squirts out of the wound.

Brooke begins to cry, and Heather drapes an arm around her.

No kidding. It's a damn good thing this truck is full of gas. We're going to be on the road for at least another couple of hours. Hopefully there's no other places we've got to worry about.

I pull into a nearby parking lot and put the truck in reverse. Two members of the undead put their hands on the truck doors. Brooke starts to cry uncontrollably, and Heather closes her eyes.

I get a cigarette out of my pocket and light it. I'm more than ready to get to the farm.

I'VE LOST track of how long I've sat here. The numbness I have in my chest doesn't seem like it's going away any time soon. I'm all out of tears since I've cried so much. Angel's gone, and he's never coming back. It's a hard pill to swallow after everything we've been through.

Get yourself together. You can't be here when it's nightfall. It's much too dangerous.

I rub my eyes and take a deep breath.

Angel would want you to get to the farm safe and sound. You've got to make him proud.

I let go of Angel's hand and make my way through the house. It's still daylight out, and hopefully I'll be able to make it to the farm by nightfall. Being on the road at night makes things so much more frightening. The darkness engulfs you, and it's hard to see. Especially if you're walking.

I open up the door to the house and see a zombie headed my way. Blood's caked on the face of what used to be a woman. The zombie must have had a meal recently. I shudder as I think about being devoured by one of them. It's such a horrible way to die.

I make a run for the car with the adrenaline pumping through my veins. My hand grabs the handle, and I hop into the driver's seat. I lock the doors, and much to my delight, the key's in the ignition.

The zombie beats on the trunk of the car, and I nearly jump out of my skin. My hands shake as I start the car. The engine roars to life, and I put the car in reverse. The zombie falls to the ground.

Anger erupts through my body as I think about Angel. I lay on the gas pedal, and the bones crunch as I roll over the zombie. The undead woman isn't dead yet. Her legs and arms are barely hanging onto her body. I didn't smash her head in with the tires.

I back up again, and her brains explode onto the grass. Now I can finally be on my way.

My first thoughts are to look at the gas tank. It's nearly half a tank. I just hope I'm able to get to the farm before I run out.

When I get to the city, there are people lined up on the sidewalk. They have sticks in their hands, and they are playing with zombies. I don't know why people have to be so sick. It's absolutely disgusting since zombies aren't anything to play with. One bad move, and you could be bitten or scratched. Then your entire life would be over. All of that could happen in the blink of an eye.

I reach the interstate, and my stomach drops. Cars are lined up on the road, and there's no way I can get around them. I squint my eyes and get a good look at the zombies that are about a mile away. There's a herd of them passing by cars. I'll just have to go the long way around.

I back up the car. Then make my way through to the other side of the city. A man with brown hair and hazel eyes comes running down the road. He's got a machete in his hand and has rage-filled eyes. It's like he's looking for somebody to kill. I don't know how people could be so crazy and full of so much evil.

Having the car locked and being in it is the only thing that gives me comfort. At least being in it doesn't make me an easy target to attack. As long as I keep moving, I won't become prey for either humans or zombies. It seems like that's the key to survival.

I've got to drown out the rest of the world and think about happier times. Coming to the farm with Angel helped me in so many ways. My grandmother raised me since my father was a drunk. He lived in the house with us when he wasn't in jail. Things weren't pleasant with him around. My grandmother didn't have the heart to make him leave. I understand it now since he was her son.

Being at the farm with Angel had been a great escape. It was like a breath of fresh air. The happiest times were spent at the farm. Not only was Angel good to me, his parents were also. They treated me like their very own.

Getting there in one piece is my only hope. I don't have anywhere else to go. I'm not certain who lives there now. They've got to give me a fighting chance.

CHAPTER 9
SUNNY

I TAKE the cigarette out of my mouth and put it in an old cup. The road in front of us is blocked off. A guy is standing on the road with a gun in his hands. There are several other people gathered around him. It's impossible to get through without running over the top of them.

The guy has a hat on his head and brown eyes. A smirk's on his lips, and I roll down my window to see what his deal is.

"It's past five, so that means this road belongs to us," the guy says.

Anger surges through my veins. This road doesn't belong to anyone. We should be able to pass through without any fuss about it.

I glare at him, and my body tenses. "We just need to get by. You know how it gets when it's nightfall."

The guy throws back his head and laughs. "I do realize how things get, but that doesn't mean I'm going to let you through."

Joey reaches for the gun in his jeans. "We can give you food if that's what you're after."

The guy leans into the driver's side window. I wish I could reach out and snap his fucking neck. That would put an end to this bullshit. If Heather, Brooke, and Landon weren't here, I would. I wouldn't think twice about it. This guy is a no-good piece of shit.

"That sounds like something I can reason with," the guy replies.

Joey rubs his brow and challenges the man with his eyes. "Landon's sitting behind me. He'll give you the canned food. So we can be on our way."

I watch the guy go around the truck like a hawk.

You better let us go after you get the canned food, you fucker.

A woman comes up behind the guy. Dirt is caked on her face, and she's got light brown hair that's pulled up in a bun. "Make sure you get everything. We need it a hell of a lot more than they do."

I shake my head in disgust but keep a tight lip. These people are just like the rest of us, trying to get by. There's nothing that makes them more special than us.

Landon opens up the truck door and blinks rapidly. He hands the guy the canned food but doesn't say anything to him. To be honest, there's nothing to be said.

You're doing good, kid. Just keep handing him the food. We'll soon be on our way.

A grin's plastered on the guy's face as he takes what's ours. "Where are you all headed?"

"Wise County," Joey lies through his teeth.

We can't let these people know we're headed to Dickenson County. They could potentially follow us there and try to overtake the farm. It wouldn't be wise to be honest with them.

The guy backs up away from the truck and shuts Landon's door. "I'll be seeing you all later."

Yeah, and you'll be dead in your fucking grave.

The people that are standing across the road move out of the way so we can pass.

I drive past them, and a tension forms in my stomach. It's

best to be cautious. They could have something else up their sleeves I don't know about.

There's nothing out of the ordinary as I drive forward. After driving for a couple of minutes, their faces disappear out of sight. I utter a sigh of relief since we're all safe and sound. That could've went bad in a heartbeat. I'm just glad it didn't.

Landon slumps his shoulders and leans his head into the passenger seat. "What the fuck is wrong with them? Now we're going to have to go on another run soon."

Brooke folds her arms across her chest. "Maybe you should ask Joey. He's the one who suggested they take the food. This is his fault and no one else's."

My patience is wearing thin, and I've had it with her. "I wasn't about to turn back around, and what Joey did kept the peace. So don't you for a minute say this is his fault. You need to shut that mouth of yours if you haven't got anything good to say."

Brooke sticks out her bottom lip in a pout. "I just want to get out of this truck!"

"Just lay your head on my lap. We'll be at the farm soon," Heather says.

Joey glances out the window. "That's the reason I went and got the two of you. Soon these roads aren't going to be safe to travel on."

I get a cigarette out of my pocket and light it. "If I was you Brooke, I'd quit bitching about Joey and be grateful you have him. He didn't have to go get the two of you."

Joey's a good man and always has been. Even if he did have a drinking problem. It's not like we're all perfect. Each one of us has flaws, and drinking was his.

Hell, he's a better man than I am. I would have left the two of them where they were. He doesn't have obligations to them anymore, since him and Heather divorced.

Brooke's eyes flutter shut, and she pretends to be asleep.

Heather clears her throat. "I'm sorry for what I said back there at the grocery store. I didn't mean it. If I had things my way, we would still be married."

I hope he doesn't lean into this shit. The two of them don't need to make up. Their divorce was finalized before the apocalypse started. Now isn't the time for them to make amends.

Joey folds his arms across his chest. "It's alright. I'm sorry for getting so heated. We were just in a bad spot. I guess I needed someone to blame."

I take a drag and then blow out smoke. Wish they'd talk about something else. This isn't something I want to hear.

Landon chimes in and changes the subject. "Why did you lie to that man back there?"

This kid has a lot to learn in this world. He's probably not been off the farm.

"We can't have people coming to the farm. They might try to slit our throats while we sleep," I answer before Joey can say anything.

Landon wrinkles his brow and bites down on his lower lip. "I guess you're saying we can't trust anyone."

"No, son, we can't," Joey replies.

CHAPTER 10
AVA

THE CAR COMPLETELY DIES, and I press a palm against my chest. It's completely dark out, and I still have another mile to go before I get to the farm. While I was on the road, I noticed a flashlight on the floor of the passenger seat.

I lean down and run my hand over the floor to retrieve it. I grab hold of it and turn it on, and the light beams out of it. Thank God it works.

I open the door to the car and step out into the darkness. My heart hammers out of my chest, and I shine the flashlight all around me. A leaf crackles, and the hairs on the back of my neck stand up.

Come out so I can see you. Don't hide from me. I'm ready to take you the fuck down.

I shine my light in the woods, and my gaze lands on a deer. The four-legged creature is brown with white spots. When our eyes meet, it takes off running away from me.

Easy now. It was only a deer. Keep going. You're almost there. Don't let this slow you down.

A gunshot goes off in the distance, and it's then I realize I'm not alone. I hadn't seen any of the undead or any people on the back road to get here. The thought of people being so close by now doesn't sit well with me. Not after everything I've experienced today.

Another gunshot echoes through the mountain, and sweat drips down my forehead. I don't know what the fuck's going on. I've got to get to the farm in one piece.

I put the flashlight in my pants and take off running as fast as I can. My shoes crunch against the rocks as I gather speed. I pump my arms at my side, and the water trickles down the waterfall.

You've got less than half a mile left. Keep going.

An uneasiness forms over me at the uncertainty of what is ahead. I've not been here ever since high school.

Don't you dare think the worst. You've come so far. You can't go back now.

I get my flashlight out of my pants and shine it in front of me. This place is just like it was the last time I was here so many years ago. My eyes land on where the house used to be.I let out a sigh of relief when I shine the light on the newly built house. Now it's a brick house with brown trim. The hardest part is over. Now to step inside. Hopefully, if anyone lives here, they will let me stay.

I don't even want to begin to think about someone not living here. If I'm here all alone, I don't know what to do. We're so far back in the mountain and away from everything that it would be like a death sentence.

I don't have a car anymore, and it would take me all day to get to town and back. Not to mention that gun being fired. An ache forms in the back of my throat as I think about having a run-in with someone. I can't leave this house. Being on my own would be so hard. Too hard, and I'm not sure I would be able to make it out alive.

I open the door to the house and step inside. The living room is fully furnished, and a blanket is draped over one of the couches. Bleach fills the room, making it certain someone has been here recently. If someone lives here, where are they now?

The kitchen's small but roomy. There's a table in the corner of the room. I open up the fridge and freezer. They're both completely empty. A picture that hangs on the wall catches my eye.

I step over to the picture and glance at it. A man's smile lights it up. He's attractive with short brown hair and a clean-shaven face. A younger guy stands beside him. The two of them both have round green eyes. Which leads me to believe they might be related.

This house probably belongs to the older man. He's going to be the one I have to convince if I want to stay. If he comes back.

I make my way up the stairs. My heart beats out of my chest as fear ignites. I have no idea what I'm going to come across. So I've got to be ready for anything.

Nausea rises in my throat, and panic sets in. What if one of the undead is in here? My knife's in my pocket, and it's all I've got. It would be difficult to take more than one of them down.

I duck into the first bedroom I come to and shut the door behind me. I'm exhausted from the journey. It's now dark out, and I don't want to leave. I've got nowhere else to go but here. Being here is my best chance at survival.

What if whoever owns this house is an asshole? I don't know him or what he's going to do. He could be like the man who wanted to kill me and Angel earlier. The unknown is what's crippling me.

I open the door to the closet and duck inside. I pull back the clothes and don't see anything alarming. There's a duffle bag full of guns, and I scoot it over to the side. The undead isn't here, or I would hear the growls erupt from their lips. Now, it's hoping that the living is good. Because if they're not,

I came all of this way for nothing. It would take a heartless man to make me leave.

I press my head against the wall. My body shakes with anticipation of what's going to come next.

CHAPTER 11
JOEY

I NOTICE the car sitting on the side of the road, and an uneasiness forms over me. The car wasn't sitting there when we left earlier. We're so far back in the mountains and away from everything that this isn't a coincidence. I rub my hand against my pants and tap my feet on the floorboard. If there's anyone here at my house, there better be a good reason for it.

I clear my throat. "Before anybody sets foot in the house, me and Sunny are looking everything over."

Sunny wrinkles his nose and grips the steering wheel. He knows something is up, but I'm not telling him what in front of everyone. "You can never be too careful."

"What are we going to do about food?" There's urgency in Landon's voice.

I haven't forgotten about him being hungry. "We'll go out searching for something in the next couple of days."

We've still got a couple of cans of food left. It will be enough for today and tomorrow at least.

I'm not putting the lives I care about at risk. There's no reason to when it won't take long to look everything over.

My palms are sweaty, and my entire body tingles. We'll be at the house within minutes. I just hope it's completely empty. We've all had a long day, and it would be nice to settle down.

Regardless of that, me and Sunny are going to keep watch tonight. Whoever was driving that car can't be far.

I stare out into the night sky and know that before I act as a lookout tonight, I'm going to need some alone time. Now that everyone's here, I just need to clear my head and think. We've got to get a handle on the way things on the farm are going to go. We're all going to have chores and things we need to know. I didn't go get Heather and Brooke so they could sit on their asses all day. They are able bodies who can help out with things.

Sunny pulls into the driveway, and I nearly jump out of the truck. This place will always be home sweet home to me. The best thing about living here is being so far away from other people.

"Feels good to be back," Landon says, opening the door to the truck.

He loves living here as much as I do and always has.

The minute that I'm out of the truck, Heather comes over to me. "I was wondering if the two of us could talk." Urgency is in her voice when she speaks.

There's nothing to talk about with you. I'll always love you, but the two of us are through.

I raise my eyebrows and tilt my head to the night sky. "We can talk first thing tomorrow. I'm sure you're probably every bit as exhausted as I am."

Even though you're not going to like what I have to say.

Heather's face falls, but she doesn't push the issue further. "Of course I am. It will be nice to have a good night's sleep."

Timmy gets down out of the truck, and I go over to him. He's got his hands out in front of him like earlier. "I don't mean you or anyone else any harm, I swear. I'll be on my way in the next couple of days."

I clench my fists at my side. "You try anything with anyone here, you're a fucking dead man."

Timmy steps back away from me. "I understand you plainly."

Sunny takes off up the porch steps. "I'm taking the downstairs. You go upstairs."

I'm two steps behind him, and everyone else follows behind me.

The very first thing I do when I get in the house is light a candle. It's pitch black and I've got to have some light. I make my way up the steps and a tenseness forms in my stomach at what lies ahead.

Today hasn't been anything what I expected it to be. Those people being at that grocery store was a wake-up call to me. There's people out there who are seeking control of what's left. We've got to be more careful wherever we go.

I go past my bedroom and walk into the bathroom. The room is just like we left it. I've got to pull back the shower curtain just to be sure. An ache forms in the back of my throat.

If someone was in here you'd be able to notice it.

I pull back the shower curtain and let out a sigh of relief. It's completely empty, no one is in here.

I stroll into the guest bedroom that's completely empty. This room used to be Brooke's before she moved out. She took her bed, dresser, and everything with her when she left. I've just not got around to adding any furniture. The closet door is open and I step inside it. There's nothing in here. Now it's finally time to go to my bedroom.

I shut the door behind me when I walk into my bedroom. The closet door is the first thing to catch my eye. It's not completely closed shut. My pulse increases, and as I ease my way closer to the closet, I hear breathing.

You better make it clear why you didn't show yourself. It's only going to take one bullet for me to end you.

I set down the candle on the nightstand, then open up the door to the closet, and come face-to-face with a woman. I cock back my gun. "Who the fuck are you, and what are you doing here?"

Her brown eyes go wide, and she steps out of the closet. "Please don't hurt me. I had nowhere to go. My friend Angel's the one who suggested coming here."

I keep my gun trained on her. I'm not ready to set it down yet. Not until a few things are clear. "Your friend Angel, where's he at now?"

She stutters on her words. "He's dead."

That would be the reason she looks so sad.

I give her an understanding nod and set my gun down on the end table. "I'm sorry about your friend."

Tears stream down her face, and she pushes them away with her hand. "He was bitten by a zombie today, and I had to end him."

That's tough, and my heart breaks for her. She must be all alone.

What's another person being here going to hurt?

"Where is it that you came from?" I ask.

"Eagleton. I've been through hell and back to get here. Please don't make me leave." She sits down on the bed, and I gaze into her sad brown eyes. My stomach flutters at the intensity of our gaze. It's been a year since I've been with a woman. Even then, that woman wasn't as attractive as this one.

I divert my gaze away from her. "I'm not going to make you go back out there. I do have to warn you that there's a house full of people here."

She lets out a sigh of relief before throwing her arms around me and giving me a hug. I'm fully aware of her breasts against my chest. My erection throbs as I picture myself touching those luscious breasts and having my way with her.

"Thank you so much for letting me stay. I'm sorry if I

frightened you by being in the closet. I just didn't know what to expect."

You're not supposed to feel this way about her. You don't want to make things awkward with Heather and Brooke.

I pull away from her. "You didn't frighten me. I just didn't want to kill you since my son's here."

She gazes away from me uncomfortably. "Please don't tell me you're like that man from earlier today."

I put my hands on the side of her face, forcing her to stare into my eyes. There's a fire burning inside me. The flames were ignited the minute I saw her. "I promise you I'm nothing like that man from earlier."

She pulls away from me. "Good. I don't want to die at the hands of a psychopath."

I lean back against the headboard and rub the bridge of my nose. "You didn't tell me your name."

"My name's Ava, and what's yours?"

"I'm Joey, and it's good to have you here."

Ava gets up from the bed to leave. "I'm going to find a place to go sleep."

"Don't—" I interrupt her.

There's no other bedrooms for her to sleep in. Not unless she sleeps on the couch, and I'm not having that.

She turns around and faces me. Her cheeks are a rosy red. "Did you have a particular place for me to sleep in mind?"

"You can stay here in my room." I fold my arms across my chest. "I've got to go back out there and keep watch."

Her eyebrows draw together, and she leans in closer to me. There's freckles on her cheeks, and they make her so much cuter. "I'm guessing this house belongs to you," she says.

I came up here fully intending on being alone. Talking to her is so much better than that.

"It does belong to me and has for the last year."

"It's so much bigger than the house that was here before."

The house that was here before was an older house with a lot of mold on the inside. I didn't have any other choice but to tear it down.

I lace my fingers behind my head as the tension of the day goes away. "I'm happy you decided to come back."

She lowers her head and parts her lips. "I was worried that everything wasn't going to be like it was the last time I was here."

I grin. "Everything's the same except for this house."

I hadn't got around to getting cows or horses yet. Was planning on getting some this summer after I had put up some fences. Guess that's not going to happen anymore.

A frown appears on her face. "There's something you should know."

Judging by the expression on her face, this can't be good. If she was hiding something from me, I would've sensed it by now.

My eyebrows draw together, and I nod, urging her to continue.

She fidgets with the hem of her shirt. "I heard gunshots about a mile from here."

It's alarming knowing other people are around. First thing tomorrow morning, I'm going to take a look around. To check on Henry and his family, to make sure they're okay.

The knocks on the door put an end to our conversation. My gaze shifts to the door, and I wonder who it is. "Come on in," I say.

Sunny steps inside the door and takes a step back when his eyes land on Ava. I give him a warning gaze. "Everybody's all settled in, and I'm going to head out to the camper," Sunny says.

Which means it's time for the two of us to talk. "I'll be out there in less than five minutes."

Sunny shakes his head. "You sure as hell have got some explaining to do."

He doesn't give me a chance to respond, since he shuts the door behind him on his way out.

She clears her throat. "Have you had problems here with other people?" Her voice is shaky.

"No, we haven't had any problems with anyone so far other than you," I joke.

She has a sparkle in her eye, and laughter erupts from her lips. "I promise to keep things on the down-low."

I grin. "There's no doubt in my mind that you will."

She presses her head against my chest, and I rub her back. I take the hair bow out of her hair, and it's a knotty mess. I run my fingers through her hair, wishing I had a hairbrush.

"It's been a long day, and I just need you to let me know everything's going to be okay," she says.

I pull back away from her. "Everything's going to be just fine. Trust me. I won't let anything happen to you."

She lies down against the bed and closes her eyes. "Can you stay in here with me until I go to sleep?"

I press a kiss against her forehead. "I promise I'm not going anywhere."

Several minutes later, she begins to snore, and I get up off the bed. Now's the time to talk to Sunny and make a plan for tomorrow. It worries me that shots were being fired. We've got to be ready for them if they do come. The last thing they're going to do is sneak up on us.

I SPOTTED the old camper on the hill down below the house. It's the perfect spot to watch for the undead. They might not be around, but that's bound to change. Being here probably isn't going to be all rainbows and butterflies. The more humanity dies out, the closer they'll come, since they don't have nothing to eat.

The moon casts light on the ground. Not enough light to give me comfort. It's the reason why I have a pistol in my hand. Can't ever be too careful with the possibility of the undead being around.

I step inside of the camper. There doesn't appear to be anything out of the ordinary. I make my way through it, step on the ladder, and stare up at the night sky. It seems like there's a million stars staring down back at me.

I open up my pack of cigarettes and light one. My body relaxes when I inhale and take that first puff. Being around all of these people has really done me in. It's nothing I have against any of them. This just isn't something I'm used to since I'm a loner.

The sound of footsteps causes me to look all around. My eyes land on Joey, who's finally come outside. It's about damn time. He said he'd be out here in a couple of minutes, fifteen minutes ago.

"She's completely harmless, and her name is Ava," he says.

I take another puff off my cigarette. "Do you know anything about her?"

He gets inside the camper, then steps up and sits beside me. "Nothing other than she's scared and needs somewhere to go."

You're a fucking dumbass. Heather and Brooke are going to be pissed about the other woman being here.

"You do realize her being here is going to get a lot of shit stirred up."

He clenches his teeth. "I'm talking to Heather tomorrow and making it clear we're through."

I flick my cigarette onto the ground. "That's going to go over well."

He rolls his eyes. "They wouldn't have survived if I hadn't went and got them when I did. It was the right thing to do."

I shrug. "Whatever you say, man. I've not forgotten how we came back from Iraq, and you found her in bed with another guy. You don't owe either one of them anything."

Heather is a bitch who brought out the worst in Joey. He got into bar fights and drank himself silly over her. When at the end of the day, nothing was worth it.

A car's headlights on the other side of the river spark my attention. The first thought that comes to mind is those people we had a run-in with earlier. What if they followed us out here?

He rocks in place and then finally stands up. "I'm going crazy with everything that's going on. There's no way I'm going to be able to get any rest tonight."

I wonder if there's something else he's not telling me. Then quickly dismiss that thought out of my mind. He's one of my truest friends and wouldn't hide anything from me.

I wrinkle my nose. "Did Ava come with any baggage?"

"She told me she heard gunshots not far away from here," he answers.

"You and I both know it would be unwise to go out there tonight. We'll keep an eye on things here. First thing tomorrow, we'll go looking for the source," I say.

There's no reason to go trampling around in the woods right now. Everyone else is asleep, and leaving could potentially be dangerous. Someone could very well be waiting in the shadows for us to leave.

"You can get some shut-eye if you want."

"I've had a long couple of days. I think I'm going to take you up on that."

———

I stare back at Nathan with a grin on my face. "What do you say about going to the movies tomorrow night?"

Nathan giggles. "Daddy. We can't go to the movies tomorrow. It's my birthday party."

I couldn't ever forget about his birthday. He's the best thing to ever happen to me.

"What do you say about going to the movies after your birthday party?" I ask.

Doing that seems like a pretty good idea.

Nathan opens his mouth to respond.

The headlights come out of nowhere. Before I have a chance to react, another car rams into the back seat.

My head crashes into the windshield, and blood rushes out of the gash. "Nathan!" I scream.

Nathan doesn't say anything back. I turn around and see his lifeless body before my eyes.

I open up my eyes, and tears stream down my face. I hate reliving these memories. Every day for the past three months, I've been having dreams about him. I've come to the conclusion that it's because I need to let him go. But letting him go is so hard. He will always be my little boy.

Joey's wide awake beside me. "Is there something you want to talk about?"

Get ahold of yourself.

I push the tears away with my hand. "I've got to go take a piss."

"Just know I'll always be around when you need to talk."

Not once has he asked me about what happened with Nathan. That's why he's always been one of my best buddies. Never has he tried to pry information out of me before. He realizes I'll talk when I need to.

I climb down below, not wanting to hear another word from him. The only thing I want is to be alone.

I stomp through the camper and start walking in the opposite direction of him. Once I'm a couple of yards away, I pull down my pants to piss. This isn't how I wanted tonight to go. I hate crying, especially in front of Joey.

I can still hear Damon's bones crunching. It wouldn't be so bad if I felt something. I feel absolutely nothing. In some sick and twisted way, I just thought it would bring me closure. It didn't bring me anything. I don't have my little boy back.

THE DOOR OPENS to the house, and Heather steps out. Her long black hair is up in a ponytail. She licks her lips, and the two of us lock eyes.

I hate to be the bad guy here. This is going to end in an argument, and I can't help it.

Sunny stretches out his arms beside me. "You two need to be alone. I'm going to get breakfast started."

Being alone is what I fully intended on doing. This isn't really a conversation for another person to hear.

I step down off the camper and stroll through it. A sour taste forms in my mouth, and I cringe, thinking about what Sunny said last night. All of those things were spot on, and he's right. There's no reason for me to give her a second chance. One chance is more than enough.

Heather is waiting for me when I step out of the camper. She blinks a mile a minute. "You said we could talk today, and that's what I fully intend on doing."

My body tingles all over, and I can't understand why she can hope for us to get back together. "Let's go talk out there by the outhouse. The two of us need to be alone."

Heather follows alongside me, and she tries to grab ahold of my hand. I put my hand in my jean pocket, out of her reach. She slumps her shoulders as we walk, and an unreadable expression is on her face.

You're making the right decision by not getting back together with her.

Ava crosses my mind and how I was such at ease with her last night. Heat radiates through my chest, and I'm eager to learn more about her.

When we're a safe distance away from Sunny, is when I stare into her eyes. It's almost as if she knows what I'm going to say. Her blue eyes are full of hurt, and I'm going to give her an explanation.

"I came to get you yesterday because I care about you," I begin to say.

I will always love you too. We were together for seventeen years.

Heather bites down on her lower lip. "I can't understand this. For the past three months, you came to check in on us. What about that has changed now?"

I run my hands through my hair, and exhaustion sets in. "What changed is crazy people have come out of hiding. This world's getting difficult to live in for people who are innocent."

Her lips turn down in a frown. "Well then, it just makes sense for the two of us to be together. I don't know how you can't see that."

The two of us had our time, and it wasn't meant to be. It's time to take a chance on someone else. Someone new. Someone I don't have baggage with.

My eye twitches, and I pace on the grass. "There's another woman here, and her name's Ava. I just thought you should know."

She takes a step back from me and shakes her head. "I can't fucking believe this! How could you bring me here with another woman?"

I force a laugh, and my pulse quickens. "You are out of

your fucking mind! She showed up last night and is trying to get by like the rest of us."

Her hand smacks into my arm, and my temper rises. "You're nothing but a fucking liar," she says.

This is the reason the two of us would never work out. There's no trust when it comes to our relationship. You can't be in a relationship like that. You'll never be happy.

She tries to slap my arm again, but I grab her hand. I'm not going to let her hit me again. No matter how angry she is with me. I don't deserve to be hit since I've done nothing wrong. "I would never lie about something like this," I snap.

She jerks away from me and begins walking back to the house. "I'm with Brooke and wish we would have never left that apartment. It would've saved me a world full of heartache."

You don't have any reason to feel guilty. There was never an indicator you were going to get back together.

I watch her stomp back to the house. I have never felt better, getting that off my chest. There might be tension between the two of us, but it's better than her seeing Ava for herself. This way she isn't surprised about anyone else being here.

Now I can go see Ava and let her know what to expect. Maybe she's up by now.

Sunny's already got a fire going in the fire pit. He's got a smirk on his face but doesn't say anything.

Fucking asshole.

He's getting enjoyment out of this.

I open up the door to the house, and Landon walks into the kitchen. There's dark circles underneath his eyes. He must not have gotten much sleep.

"We're heading out to Henry's as soon as we eat breakfast. Go get yourself something. Sunny's cooking," I say.

Landon yawns and gives me a nod of approval. "Sounds good. I'm absolutely starving."

I head up the stairs, and my body buzzes with excitement. I didn't get any sleep last night, but right now I feel alive.

Electricity flies off my hand when I touch the doorknob.

Now I will finally be able to see Ava.

I open the door, and Ava rolls over in bed to stare at me. Her hair may be disheveled, but she looks adorable. "How did you sleep last night?" I move closer to the bed and sit down.

She gives me a small smile. "I slept okay."

I meant what I said about keeping you safe. Nobody's going to hurt you. They'll have to go through me first.

"There's a few things we need to talk about before we have breakfast."

She sits up in bed and runs a hand across her cheekbone. "Okay…"

I reach out and squeeze the inside of her thigh. Heat floods her face, and my insides go wild. It couldn't be any more apparent that the two of us have a connection. "My ex-wife and stepdaughter are both here."

She wrinkles her brow and backs up away from me. "Is it such a good idea, me sleeping in here then?"

I'm not letting them get in the way of my happiness.

"It's perfectly fine. The two of them are just going to get over it."

Her body relaxes, and then she leans her head against the headboard. "I just don't want to overstep any boundaries with you."

You're not overstepping anything. The two of us haven't even fucked yet.

I wonder what she looks like underneath those clothes. Fucking her would take all the stress away.

"I'm a divorced man for a reason," I reassure her.

Her face softens, and a hint of a smile reaches her eyes. "I was married for ten years and divorced too."

I wonder what happened with her marriage. There's got to

be a reason for it, other than love not being enough. "I'm not proud of the man I used to be back then. I've changed a lot ever since my marriage ended. Changes that have made me better for it."

She stares into my eyes so intently that I want to close the distance between the two of us. I have every aching desire to kiss her lips and have my way with her. "I had three miscarriages, and the guy got upset I couldn't carry his child. Was one of the hardest times of my life."

That guy was a fucking idiot. There's more to a marriage than having children. Not everyone is blessed with God's miracles.

I wrap my arm around her shoulders to give her comfort. "My son is the best thing to ever happen to me. He came as a surprise. If a woman couldn't have my kid, you best believe I would cherish the blessings we did have."

She has a twinkle in her eye when she looks up at me. "That's sweet for you to say. It's just too bad not everyone is that way."

I tap her on the nose. "The only person who matters is the person you're in a relationship with."

Her stomach begins to growl, and she laughs. "Guess it's been a while since I ate anything."

I grab ahold of her hand. "Breakfast is ready. So let's go outside and eat."

CHAPTER 14
AVA

I FOLLOW Joey in the hallway, my nerves getting the best of me. He was so nice to me last night despite the fact that I was hiding in the closet. I hope everyone is as nice to me as he has been.

Joey squeezes my hand, and it gives me comfort knowing he's right by my side. I wouldn't want to face everyone all alone. There's no telling what they would try to do to me.

You shouldn't think about what everyone else has to say. This is Joey's house.

We walk down the steps, and my breath catches in my throat.

Relax. Joey's not going to let anything happen to you.

A young woman with coal-black hair meets us at the door. "Who the fuck are you?"

Her tone irritates me, but I try not to let it get underneath my skin. "My name's Ava, and who are you?"

Joey lets go of my hand and narrows his eyes at her. "This is Brooke. She used to be my stepdaughter."

So that would be the reason she acted so rude.

Brooke stares at me, her eyes full of rage. "You had no right to be in Joey's room."

Confusion sets in at what she's saying. "The two of us didn't do anything sexual if that's what you're implying."

Brooke pushes past the two of us and goes outside. I don't know what her problem is. I'm not looking forward to being here with her for however long. If Joey was together with someone, he would have mentioned it last night.

Joey turns to me, and my heart flutters as I stare into his green eyes. Not only is he nice, but he's handsome. "She hates me since I brought her here yesterday. Don't let her get underneath your skin."

I wouldn't say she hates me right now. I just don't think she likes me at all. There's nothing I can do about that. I'm not leaving this farm unless Joey makes me. I'm almost certain that he won't.

I force a smile. "I'll try not to. Let's go see everyone else."

This is going to be harder than what I imagined it to be. I just hope everyone isn't going to be like her. I'm eager to meet the rest of the people who I will be living with.

Joey opens the door, and I step outside beside him. The sun shines down on me, and it's going to be a hot day. My eyes catch sight of two people huddled around the fire pit.

Growls escape from my stomach, and I can't wait to get me something to eat. Joey doesn't leave my sight, and it helps get rid of my nerves.

I notice the boy that was in the picture. He's got green eyes like Joey's.

Joey gives the two of us a proper introduction. "Ava, this is my son, Landon. Landon, Ava came here last night while we were gone."

Landon's green eyes get wide, and he finishes eating his food. "Damn, Dad, you never mentioned her."

"I never mentioned her since you were already asleep," Joey says.

Landon shrugs. "Makes perfect sense."

A guy with shaggy brown hair and a graying beard is

standing by the food. I remember him coming into the bedroom last night. "I heard Joey talking, and I'm Sunny. You want some soup?" Sunny asks.

My nerves seep away since these two men seem okay with me being here. It replaces the uneasiness with happiness.

"I would love some," I answer.

Sunny dips me out a bowl of soup and hands me a spoon. "There you go. It's not a lot, but there's hardly any food in the house."

I shake my head. "It's absolutely perfect."

Joey comes over to me. "How about you go sit down? I'll join you as soon as I get me some."

I stroll over to the garage full of picnic tables and have a seat. The soup burns the inside of my mouth when I take the first bite. I'm too hungry to care and keep eating until there's no more left in my bowl.

Joey stares down at my bowl that's already completely empty. He sits his bowl of food in front of me. "Take mine. One bowl isn't going to be enough to fill you up."

As tempting as it is, I can't. He's got to eat too. There's no reason for me to be greedy by taking his. This is just how things have to be until we go out on another run.

"I'm fine. Thank you for being so kind," I say.

He shakes his head. "I'm not taking that for an answer. Eat it. I know you're still hungry."

I let out a sigh of frustration and reluctantly take the bowl. "You didn't have to do that for me."

He leans forward, so close our noses almost touch. Warmth radiates through my body, and my cheeks are on fire. This beautiful man is staring back at me, and I'm tempted to kiss his lips.

"You're wrong. I did. I'm not having you going hungry."

"Where is it that you bathe?" Curiosity gets the best of me.

He grins. "In the river, and I'll let you borrow some of my clothes."

It makes perfect sense bathing in the river. I should've known to think of that. I'm going to have to bathe in the river sometime soon. It's been two days since I've washed off.

I push the bowl of soup back in front of him. There's no way I'm letting him go hungry because of me. "Do you have a toothbrush I can use?"

He laughs. "I've got an extra one back in the house I'll let you have."

I can't stand a day going without brushing my teeth. It makes my mouth feel dirty. So that's good to know. Once we go back up to the house, I'll get it from him. "This might seem like a stupid question. I've got to empty my bladder."

He points at an outhouse a few yards away. "The outhouse came with this property when I bought it last year."

I give him a small smile. "I know exactly where it is. I'm just glad you didn't get rid of it."

He folds his arms across his chest. "I'm glad I didn't either. We need it more than anything now."

I get up from the picnic table and walk up onto the hill. My bladder feels like it's going to explode any minute.

I reach the outbuilding, and the smell overwhelms me. Somebody must have taken a shit a couple of minutes ago. The smell's overbearing, and nausea sets in. I swallow back down the throw-up.

I spot a tree and duck behind it so I remain out of sight. I pull down my pants and empty the contents of my bladder. Relief washes over me as I let the pee trickle down onto the rocks.

A man walks out of the woods and stares at me. "I've always had bladder problems."

I pull my pants back up. "It's something you can't help, and I'm fine now."

The man takes a good look at me. I scrunch my nose since

he smells so damn bad. "I'm going to go bathe. You're the prettiest thing I've seen in a while. Do you care to join me?"

I drop my hands to my sides and gape at him. First he takes a shit in the outhouse that stinks to high heavens. Then he creeps up on me unannounced while I'm taking a piss. What the fuck is wrong with him?

"I think I'll pass on that."

Disappointment is written on his face. "I'm sure Sunny or Joey will be my lookout then."

Joey comes up to where the two of us are standing. I wonder how much of it he's seen or heard. "Is everything alright?" Joey asks.

You being here has made everything better.

I grin. "Everything's just fine."

A woman who appears in her early forties comes out of the house and glares at me. "Nice, you were the one sleeping in my ex-husband's room. It didn't take long for the two of you to fuck. You should be proud of yourself, Joey."

This must be his ex-wife.

Joey shakes his head. The annoyance is written all over his face. "The two of us didn't fuck. Not that it's any of your business. You're really going to bitch about this? After everything I went through yesterday to get you here?"

I'm at a loss for words. There's no reason for anyone to be hostile towards me. I didn't make any moves on Joey. I have to know this is what I really want before I do something like that.

Landon lets out a sigh in frustration. "Can't we all just get along? If dad was fucking someone, I would be the first to know."

Sunny grabs ahold of my hand and leads me away from them. The two of us begin walking down the road. "I'm glad you're here. Don't worry about those other bitches. The entire ride home yesterday was spent listening to them. Wanted to leave them on the damn side of the road."

I laugh. "It's good knowing someone other than Joey wants me here."

Sunny stops walking, and I do too.

I don't want us wandering too far away from everybody. You looked on the verge of getting upset back there, and they're not even worth it."

It would just be nice to be around a group of survivors where we all got along. So much for that, since it's apparently not going to happen.

"Thank you for helping to give me peace of mind," I say.

He pats me on the shoulder. "I'm just looking out for you. I was out there all alone myself. It sucks major ass not having anybody to talk to. Then you start talking to yourself like you're some sort of crazy person."

A lump forms in my throat as I think about Angel. He didn't deserve to go out the way he did. "I wouldn't be able to survive if I didn't have anyone to talk to."

The two of us begin walking back. "I feel the exact same way you do."

We round the bend, and a zombie floats down in the water. The body washes away downstream. I shudder, and fear shoots through my body. There's no way I'm bathing in the water today. I'll save that for tomorrow. If there's one in there, I'm certain there's more.

I stammer on my words. "I just saw a zombie floating in the water."

He puts his arm around my shoulder. "I'm not surprised since there's people around."

Thinking about those men trying to murder me yesterday makes me sick. I can only think the worst about people. Being here with Joey and Sunny is where I completely lucked out.

Joey's ex-wife is nowhere to be seen. She may have disappeared back into the house. Either way I'm not worried about her. To be honest, I'm glad she's not around.

Joey narrows his eyes at me. "Is everything okay? You look like you've seen a ghost or something."

"I saw a zombie in the river," I say.

"Son of a fucking bitch. We've got to keep our eyes open. I'm going to go check on a friend of mine." Joey stares intently into my eyes. My heart skips a beat. "I was hoping you would go with me."

I can't stand to stay here with those other two women. "Of course I will. Just let me know when you're leaving."

Joey's face lights up. "Right now, if you're up for it."

"Alright then. Let's go."

I WALK UP the house's front steps to get Landon. He went inside to put on a pair of shorts. There's no way I'm making a trip or going anywhere without him. I won't be able to protect him if I'm not around him.

Sunny may not like Heather or Brooke, but they'll be fine here together. I don't want Heather or Brooke to be alone with Timmy. He's a stranger, and I can't say that I trust him.

Heather's sitting down at the table when I walk through the door. "I can't believe you. Having another woman in your bedroom that could potentially be a threat to all of us."

My blood boils at what she's saying. Ava's not a threat to anyone. If she was, I'd make sure her ass was gone before morning.

This is nothing but bullshit. "I can have whoever the fuck I want here. This house belongs to me. Don't even get me started with this shit."

Heather shakes her head in disgust. "You don't get to make those decisions without asking all of us first. We all live here together. It's not just you."

I press my lips together and clench my fist. Landon needs to hurry up. I'm done with talking to her. "We're having a meeting when I get back. Just so we're clear about things."

Landon stands between the two of us. "Come on, old man. Let's get going."

I follow him out the door, happy to be out of Heather's sight.

Ava's standing outside with her arms across her chest when Landon and I come out of the house. "So where are we headed?" Ava asks.

"To a man's house that me and Landon know," I say.

The three of us start on our journey to Henry's house. It will be no more than a thirty-minute walk if things go as planned. There's no reason to use Sunny's truck since we're not going far at all.

Landon peers at me and then Ava. "I'm curious. Did you two fuck last night?"

I swallow back my laughter. "The two of us barely know each other. You should be able to answer that question yourself."

Ava's cheeks turn rosy red. "I would have introduced myself to everybody last night. It's just that I was scared and didn't know what to expect."

Landon shrugs. "You had a reason to be scared. My dad here is an asshole."

I would never intentionally be an asshole towards Ava.

Ava takes a deep breath and bends over. "I need to rest just for a minute."

I touch her arm and stare at her with concern. "Are you alright?"

Ava nods. "It's just hot out here."

Landon walks up ahead of us a couple of steps. "This heat is something we better get used to. Summer's just beginning."

It makes me wish I would've got some horses back in the spring. I just didn't want the hassle of taking care of them. Buying them feed and water would add up after a while. Money I could have spent somewhere else.

"Maybe we can find a car and drive it back," I joke.

I'm still pissed off about the car being stolen yesterday. All because of Heather and Brooke. They've been rude to Ava for no good reason. I refuse to let them make things awkward for her. My farm's big enough for all of us to stay there.

Ava begins to walk, and I'm right beside her. "Wouldn't that be something," she replies.

There's a zombie up ahead in Darren's yard. The undead looks up at me, and it's him. His eyes are red. A pit forms in my stomach. Just last week I've seen him. He was doing just fine.

"We've got to be cautious," I announce.

Ava's face gets two shades whiter. "Didn't realize the undead were so close."

I put my arm around her shoulder. "We can go back if you want."

Ava shakes her head. "I can't go back. You two are on a journey out here. I fully intend to join you. This is good for me."

I take the knife and plunge into Darren's head, putting him out of his misery.

"Can't believe he's gone. I've spent more time at his house than yours, old man," Landon says.

Ava's hand touches mine, and I put my fingers through hers. This is just something that feels right. "Why's that?"

Landon's lips turn down in a frown. "I was together with his daughter. She went away to college last year, and I haven't seen her since."

"I'm sorry," Ava says.

"I hate to break it to you, son, but I'm not. She left without saying goodbye. It's pretty fucking shitty if you ask me," I answer.

Thinking about her makes my blood boil. I don't like seeing my son hurt, and she did a number on him. He got drunk almost every weekend when she left. His world fell apart, and there was nothing I could do to help him.

Landon picks up a rock and throws it into the river. "I can't really blame her for wanting to get away. It just sucks I didn't even get a goodbye."

"Maybe she thought it would have been easier without telling you goodbye." Ava looks deep in thought. "Especially if she loved you."

I snort. "It didn't make things easier on anyone and was the wrong thing to do."

The sound of a car engine coming down the road makes my chest tighten. The three of us duck into the woods behind a tree. Ava grips my hand, and she flares her nostrils.

I put my finger up to my lips, motioning for her to be quiet.

The little red car comes to a stop, and my heart sinks. This car belongs to Henry. I can only think the worst, and if something happened to him, it's my fault. I should've made an effort to check in on him yesterday.

A man with coal-black hair gets out of the car. He's wearing an orange jumpsuit and has tattoos all over his neck. "It's just too bad we're almost out of gas. I'm sure we can find something else along this road."

An uneasiness forms over me. I wonder who else is here with him. It won't be long before he makes his way to my farm. We've got to defend ourselves and get ready for them to come.

A woman steps out of the car. "It will make my soul happy killing everyone else in our path. That old man and his family never seen us coming."

Landon's fists clench at his side. "He didn't deserve that," he whispers.

"Shut up," I mouth to him.

The man takes the woman in his arms and gives her a passionate kiss. "We better get going now. We've got to inform everyone else. Tell them there's several more houses down this way."

I slip my hand into my pocket as I watch their every move. I want nothing more but to kill them. I'm afraid there will be a price I have to pay for their death. Not only that, but we don't know where their camp is.

The woman gets into the car and slams the door shut. The guy makes his way into the driver's side, and the two of them are on their way.

Ava's hand trembles against mine. "I'm glad I didn't come across them when I was walking yesterday. I wouldn't be alive if I did."

The veins pop out of Landon's neck. "We've got to go see if his family is still alive."

I shake my head. "It's too risky. We're going back home to warn the others."

Landon shakes his head in disgust. "I thought you were better than that, old man."

Irritation seeps through my soul. "Is it wrong of me to want to keep you alive? I would go crazy if something ever happens to you."

Landon's face softens. "It's still disappointing not knowing if any of them made it."

"Hopefully they're all just fine," I say.

CHAPTER 16
SUNNY

HEATHER AND BROOKE have been down below us eating soup. I'm glad I haven't had to listen to them bitching. It's always something with the two of them. Instead I've been listening to Timmy. Not that I can say that it's any better.

It's a good thing for me since Joey, Ava, and Landon came back several minutes ago. Now I'm just waiting for all of them to come out of the house.

Timmy just now mentioned how he wants to bathe in the river.

"I'm sure Joey will let you borrow some of his clothes," I say.

Timmy's face lightens up. "If he doesn't, I'll just have to go naked."

Not only does he smell to high heavens, but he's nastier than fuck too. Why the hell would I want to see him naked? Better yet, why would anybody?

"Believe me when I say, he's going to have clothes for you to borrow," I reassure him.

Joey comes out of the house with a troubled expression on his face. "We all need to sit down in the garage and talk."

The only thing I can come up with is something happened. That something must not have been anything good.

I walk down to the garage and have a seat at the picnic table.

Timmy sits down across from me. He pinches his throat and rubs his cheek. "This makes me worry about our safety."

I shrug. "What's worrying going to help anything? It's going to just keep you from losing focus on what you need to be doing."

Timmy takes a deep breath. "You act like you're not scared of anything."

"My family's dead, and they're not coming back." The words sting worse than any pain I've ever known, but they need to be said. Maybe if I say them enough, I'll start to accept it. "I don't have to be afraid of dying when the ones I loved most in the world are gone."

Timmy seems to understand what I'm saying. "I get your reasoning. I'm sorry you lost them."

The group moves towards us, and I let any response falter. Brooke is holding onto Heather. The two of them sit far away from me. Ava has a seat beside me, and Landon is on the other side of her.

Joey's face twists in anger. "I'm not going to stand here and talk for a long period of time. This meeting is about other people being nearby. People who have a car and are going to come out here looking. We've got to be prepared when they do."

Heather's fingers tap anxiously against her thigh. Her teeth worry her lip, and I'm afraid she might bite a hole through the damn thing. "How many of them are there?" she asks.

Joey shakes his head. "I don't know. There's at least a man and a woman. I can't be certain how many more."

Brooke stomps her foot, and her veins stand out in her neck. "Nowhere is safe. This just proves that. Fuck you, Joey, for bringing us here!"

Landon jumps up from the picnic table. "Don't you dare say that about him. We're doing the best that we can."

I light a cigarette and take a long drag, letting the tension from my body ease and disperse with my exhale. "I'll go in the woods and see what I can find. Chances are they are probably close by. We have to know what we're up against."

Ava shakes her head. "You can't go out there, Sunny. It's too risky for you to put yourself on the line for all of us."

Joey paces around the garage. "If you want to go out there and find them, I'm not going to stop you."

I spring up from the picnic table, not wanting to hear anything else. "I'll be back before nightfall."

Timmy joins me. "I'm not letting you go out there all alone."

I don't know why he's trying to look like some hero. When in reality, he's just a fucking scaredy cat. "You aren't going anywhere with me if your ass isn't clean."

Timmy turns to Joey. "Have you got any clothes I can wear?"

Joey nods. "Come up to the house, and I'll get you some."

Leaving sounds like a great idea right about now. I stay because, as much as I hate to admit it, I'll enjoy his company.

Ava walks alongside me up to the house. "Things don't have to be this way," she says.

I've already made up my mind. I'm going, and there's nothing she can do about it.

"They do have to be this way. I'm not standing here and doing nothing, waiting for these people to attack us," I reply.

Ava takes off the necklace she's wearing. "May God protect you and keep you safe."

I've never been religious, but this cross necklace gives me comfort. "I'm going to be just fine, you wait and see."

If anything does happen to me, it's not like my death would mean much. Mostly everyone else is family here. I would be taking one for the team. Not that I intend on dying.

Ava wraps her arms around me and gives me a hug. "You better. I can't bear the thought of losing someone else."

It's amazing how one person can make you feel. Not in a sexual way, but a friendly type of way. Even though we've known each other a couple of hours, she makes me feel like she cares.

"Don't you go worrying yourself over me," I say. "I promise. I'll come back."

Timmy saunters out of the house with a towel, soap, and change of clothes. "I was hoping you would still be here."

I roll my eyes. "Where the hell would I go? I'm a man who sticks to his word."

Timmy walks down the steps and onto the gravel driveway. "I'm hoping you'll be my lookout while I bathe in the river."

Of course I'll be his lookout while he bathes in the river. He better not take all damn day bathing either. We've got to get a move on.

"Who the fuck's going to watch you, the women?" I ask.

Ava crinkles her nose. "You two be safe out there."

Timmy is two steps ahead of me. "Don't worry. We will be."

I join Timmy as he makes his way down the embankment. "You be careful getting into that water."

Timmy rolls his eyes. "Don't worry. I'm going to be in and out."

As long as he puts soap on his body, it's fine by me.

Timmy pulls off his shirt, and I look away from him. Looking across the river brings my little boy to mind. How we went fishing last summer and he caught a fish. His smile lit up my entire world. I don't think I've ever seen him so happy.

Anger ignites inside of me, and the hatred comes to the surface. My little boy should still be here. He shouldn't be dead in his grave. That fucking drunk got what he deserved.

I'll never regret letting those zombies rip him apart. Serves him right for the heartache I have.

I pick up a small rock and throw it into the water.

Timmy takes a step back. "I'm trying to bathe here in case you've forgotten."

What does it fucking matter if some water splashed on him? He's getting wet anyway.

"I'm sorry. Just thinking about things," I say.

Timmy's silent for several seconds. I turn around to make sure he's okay. He's nowhere to be seen. Worry kicks in. Nothing can happen to him. We've all got to make it out of here alive.

He comes up for air no more than a minute later. "Don't worry. I'm almost ready to get out."

"I'm not worrying about nothing," I lie through my teeth.

The zombie in the river concerns me. We've not seen it yet. So it means we've got one zombie on the property. That's one zombie too many if you ask me.

CHAPTER 17
AVA

IT HURTS my heart seeing Sunny and Timmy leave. Knowing very well they might not be coming back. I understand why they left, and begging them to stay wouldn't be the right thing to do.

I head up the stairs to Joey's bedroom so the two of us can be alone. The last thing I want is to be stuck talking to Brooke or Heather. "What are we going to do?" I ask.

Joey shakes his head. "If you're suggesting leaving, that's not going to happen. I refuse to leave this place. I've got a closet full of bullets and a gun case at the end of the hallway. That's going to keep us from going anywhere any time soon."

Those guns and bullets aren't going to last forever.

"So what, you're just going to shoot whoever comes here?" I ask.

I wish this wasn't the way life was. It will never sit right with me having to kill other people just to survive. We're all human beings, and this is the only life we get.

Joey shrugs. "I'm going to do whatever I can to keep all of us safe. I hope it doesn't come down to killing people. But you heard what that man and woman said back there. That's what we're up against."

Disgust runs through my entire body. He's right. Things

will be better when they're no longer alive. The way they talked makes it apparent they're both not good people. They're a different breed of people from the two of us.

"They wouldn't give any of us mercy." I sit down on the bed, unable to say anything else.

Joey edges his way closer to me. "No, you're right. They wouldn't. That's the exact reason we can't give them any. People are just going to keep evolving and be worse than what they are now."

I hate hearing him say it. It's like the devil unleashed his demons among us. With no consequences, all evil is coming out now. There is no one to lock a person up in prison. No one to hold court hearings for the crimes committed.

"After everything being said and done, I'm just happy I made it here," I reply.

Here might not be the greatest place in the world. But it's better than being out there on my own.

Joey stares into my eyes so intensely my insides melt. He's a sexy man who's got the prettiest green eyes I've ever seen. "You mentioned earlier you wanted to brush your teeth."

I lean forward and clutch my hands together. "I can't stand feeling like my mouth is dirty."

It makes me feel absolutely disgusting not brushing my teeth. One thing that will always matter to me is having good hygiene.

He holds out his hand, and I grab ahold of it. His calloused hands make me wonder if he's rough in bed. My entire body is on fire as I think about him putting his hands all over me. "That makes the two of us."

I follow him into the hallway and catch a glimpse of his round ass. He's muscular, and I can only imagine what he looks like naked. A part of me aches for his touch. Even though it would be crazy, since we just met yesterday. I don't have any condoms or other forms of birth control.

"Your ex-wife and Brooke don't like me," I say as the two of us walk past another bedroom.

The two of us continue walking until we get into the bathroom. He opens up the door and puts his hand on my back. I lean forward and breathe in his masculine scent. This gives me ease and peace of mind.

"I don't care what Brooke and Heather think of you. I like you, and it's the only thing that matters," he whispers.

His lips brush across my ear, and I try to catch my breath. "Why are the two of them here?" It's been weighing on my mind since this morning.

He turns his back to me and gets an unopened toothbrush out of the cabinet. "I'm going to be honest with you. I was married to Heather for seventeen years. Before the apocalypse happened, the two of us got a divorce."

I grab the toothbrush from his hand. "Is she wanting to get back together with you?" I ask.

He hands me a bottle of water and tube of toothpaste. "I made it clear earlier I didn't want any part of it. What the two of us had was in the past. Now it's time to move on. I want to get to know you."

I grin. "That's good to know. I would like to get to know you too."

His entire face lights up. "What was your life like before this?"

I nearly choke on laughter. "My life was boring. I had the same routine every day."

His green eyes make my heart smile. "You don't seem all that boring to me."

"I would go to work every day and finish my day by going to the gym. Come home and drink a glass of wine."

He puts water on his toothbrush and tops it off with toothpaste. "Sounds like a good way to spend your days to me."

"It would have been nice to have some fun every now and again."

I reflect back on my old life and wish I would've got out more. After my divorce, I spent most of my time in my house. The divorce left me devastated, and I didn't date after it.

He spits into the sink and then steps back so I can brush my teeth. "I'll tell you something, if you promise not to think I'm a bad person."

Oh no. I don't know where this is going.

I brush my teeth, enjoying how refreshed my mouth is. "You're talking crazy right now."

"After my divorce, Landon and I got drunk every other day before this apocalypse happened. I'm ashamed to admit it, but those were some good times we had. It helped numb the pain of not being married anymore."

I reach out and touch his cheekbone. "How's that wrong or crazy? The two of you were both heartbroken. Seems to me like having drinks was just the thing you needed to do."

He grabs ahold of my hand and kisses it. "I don't know. Maybe it's because he was underage when we drank so much."

I search his green eyes that are filled with nothing but heartache. Heather sure did a number on him when they were married. "The two of you are both okay. So I don't see how that matters."

He leans forward, and I think he's going to kiss me. I close my eyes, wanting so desperately for his lips to meet mine.

"It matters because I was nothing but a drunk. I should have laid off the bottle, and I didn't."

I gather his face in my hands, forcing him to look at me. "We've all made mistakes in our past. You're not drinking now, and you've kept us all safe. So I say you're doing great in my book. Not to mention, you've been good to me the time I've been here. When you didn't have to be."

His lips turn up into a grin. "You're awful sweet, you know that."

I'm only sweet when it comes to you.

"Dad! Isabella's coming our way!" Landon calls from downstairs.

Joey grabs ahold of my hand. "Isabella's our neighbor, and I've known her ever since she was a little girl. We've got to go find out what's going on."

The two of us hurry out of the bathroom, past the bedroom, and down the stairs. An abrupt knock on the door startles me, and I nearly jump out of my skin. Joey goes to answer the door.

Isabella throws her arms around Joey. "They killed everyone, and I think they plan on coming here next."

TIMMY HASN'T SHUT the hell up the entire time we've been in the woods. My suspicions are he's scared. It's apparent in the way he's been looking around and the tremors in his voice. Maybe I should have just left him back at the house. He's not got anything to prove.

"Who do you think that woman was we saw back there?" Timmy asks.

A couple of minutes ago, we saw a woman running down the road. It was almost as if she was running for her life. For all I know, she could have been. Those people can't be far.

"How the fuck would I know? I'm not from around these parts," I answer.

He stops walking and bends over. "Do you even think we're going to find anything?"

"I wouldn't have wanted to come walking if I didn't think we could." I get a cigarette out of my pocket and light it.

He blinks his eyes. "What do you think we're up against?"

I blow out smoke. "You're starting to get on my fucking nerves with these questions."

He begins walking again. "I'm sorry. I just don't know what else to say."

"How about you just be quiet for a couple minutes."

He hums in a low voice, and I shake my head. This is worse than him talking.

The two of us come to the end of the driveway. I finish off my cigarette and then slide down the hill onto the road. He comes up beside me. I get a whiff of soap and not body odor. At least he smells much better now.

He looks at me with uncertainty. "Which way are we going?"

There's a bend in the road. We can keep walking down the road we're on or go up this winding driveway that leads to a house or something.

I step onto the gravel driveway, not for any particular reason. "Here, and get your ass moving. We don't have any time to waste."

He stammers on his words. "I don't have a good feeling about this."

Which is the reason this is the right way to go. "The more you complain means the longer we're out here."

I put a hand on my gun, ready to kill any fuckers I come across. I'm not scared of pulling the trigger. Sometimes it's something that needs to be done.

The driveway is curvy, winding, and narrow. So narrow that only one vehicle would fit on it. If a car came, there's nowhere to go, other than making a jump down the hill. A jump down the hill will for sure cause a broken bone.

"Where did you live before you came here?" he asks.

Here we go with these questions again. I guess I better be happy he's not humming. The humming was the worst. Got on my last damn nerves. I'm just going to get used to the sound of his mouth running. Hopefully it won't be bad.

"I lived in Ohio and was in the process of moving to Violet Mountain before the apocalypse hit. Was looking for the chance to start over." A lump forms in my throat as I reflect back on everything.

My boy and I were supposed to be living in Brute City.

Our house didn't feel like a home anymore. Not after my wife died two years ago. Cancer took her from me. They caught it late, and she didn't last five months. It's the worst type of hell watching someone you love die before your eyes.

"I hear you with that one. Starting over is always a good thing," he says.

"That's why I'm out here right now. Family isn't something I have left."

We make our way past a pond, and getting to whatever's at the top seems promising. We've just got to make it a little while longer.

My chest tightens, and I rub the back of my neck. I wonder what's ahead of us. I hope it's something good. We deserve something good to happen to us today.

"You seem like a good person, and that's why I have to tell you something," he sounds serious.

I stop walking and part my lips. "You can tell me anything."

He lets out a sigh. "Those people were after me since I slept with some guy's girlfriend."

I can't withhold my laughter. "If you slept with my girlfriend, I would want you dead too."

I don't know what he was thinking. He's got to have more sense than that.

He puts his arms across his chest. "At least it was some good fucking sex."

I shake my head. "I'm sure it was fantastic."

This guy has serious issues. A whole lot more issues than I have.

"You said that you don't have any family." He pauses. "Do you ever miss fucking?"

Out of all the things we could be talking about, he brings this up. There's more to life than sticking my dick into a vagina. My wife was the only woman I've ever been with. A woman's going to have to be incredible to change that.

"Some of us don't need sexual pleasure from others to be satisfied," I say.

He looks at me like I'm crazy. "You're not a normal man."

I roll my eyes. "Like you fucking are."

Being normal is so overrated. I like being an outcast. There's something good about not being like everyone else.

"I'm as normal as you can get," he answers.

I stop walking when I notice the house up ahead. A car is parked in the driveway. The two of us need to proceed with caution. Dread washes over me. I don't know what to expect.

I get out my gun and hold it in front of me. "Get ready. We're going in."

His eyes go wide, and beads of sweat drip off his forehead. "I don't feel so well."

I edge my way closer to the door. "Don't be such a fucking pussy. You're the one who wanted to come."

He follows in behind me. "What kind of person would that make me if I made you come out here all alone?"

One who needs to realize I'm a man who knows how to defend himself.

I place a finger to my lips so he'll shut the fuck up. My hand turns the door handle, and I slowly open the door. My eyes land on a zombie chained up against the wall. The undead's teeth chatter, and growls erupt from its lips.

I take a step closer, and the undead reaches out its hands. The fingernails are sharp like cat claws. If I'm not careful, it would rip me to shreds in a heartbeat.

I shake my head and grimace. Whoever is here can't be like everyday society. Nobody in their right fucking mind would have a zombie chained up in their house. It makes me sick since it's disgusting.

Timmy puts a hand across his mouth and makes a gagging sound. "Do you smell that?"

Of course I smell it. How could I not? A metallic scent fills my nose, and I ease my way forward, looking for the source.

The thought of someone still being alive makes my blood boil. We've got to keep pushing forward to see where it's coming from.

"Is anyone here?" I call out.

Several seconds pass by, and I don't get an answer. There doesn't appear to be a single person alive here. The pungent aroma mixed in with metallic is enough to knock you off your feet. The aroma becomes overpowering the closer we get to the bathroom.

We reach the bathroom, and my hand's automatically on the shower curtain, getting ready to pull it back. I listen intently to see if I can hear anything. Timmy gulps down his breath beside me. A shiver runs down my spine when I pull back the shower curtain. A dead woman with long red hair stares back at me. Her green eyes will forever be frozen in time. She's stripped of her clothes and has fresh cuts on her throat.

Timmy blinks slowly, trying to absorb everything. "We've got to get out of here," he stammers on his words.

Whatever you do, try to keep Timmy alive. He didn't know what he signed up for when he came here with you.

"I'm not leaving until we know how many people are here," I snap.

I shuffle my feet and move on towards the bedroom. The bed's unmade, and there's clothes hanging up in the closet.

The front door opens, and I flex my fingers. I walk back through the house to see who this sick fuck is. A man with long gray hair steps into the living room. He's wearing a pair of boots, jeans, and a torn shirt. He walks over to the zombie. "Allie, sweet pea, Daddy's got you some more food in the bathtub."

That poor, innocent woman who didn't deserve her life taken.

I clench my fists at my side and flare my nostrils. The rage that consumes my body's dying to be let out.

Don't do it. Timmy's here with you.

"I love doing this for you, my sweet precious girl. The best part is watching their lives escape from their eyes. They die for a good reason, and that's so you can stay here with me," the man says.

Joey, Landon, Ava, Brooke, and Heather all come to mind. It could have been any of them in that bathtub. My face is on fire, and the rage comes pouring out of me. No one else is going to become a victim. I'm going to make sure of it.

I plant my feet wide and tackle the guy to the ground. A smirk settles on his face, and I have every desire to beat him dead. His fist collides with my nose, and adrenaline pumps through my body.

Timmy runs across the floor, but I don't pay him any mind. If he wants to leave, that's on him. I won't be able to help him if he runs into any trouble.

I rear back and slam my head against his. Blood pours down my face, but I don't fucking care. This fucker is getting everything coming to him. He's the one person in this world who deserves to die. Killing people so that he can feed a zombie. It's beyond sickening.

The man touches his forehead and then shows me his rotten teeth. His breath eats me alive, and I want to rip out every tooth he's got left in his mouth.

Timmy runs back into the room and plunges a knife into the man's back. "Take this, you fucking animal."

The man gets off me and turns his attention to Timmy. His brown eyes go completely black. "I wouldn't have done that if I was you."

I get my pocket knife out of my pants and slit his throat. "Shut the fuck up and go to hell where you belong."

The blade of the knife slices through skin and into his jugular. He lies on the floor and gasps for breath. I'm just going to let him suffer. It's not like he's going anywhere. He'll be dead before the hour's over with. Not unless he turns into zombie. Then I'll put him down.

Timmy's mouth falls open, and he slumps his shoulders. Several minutes pass by with silence between the two of us. "We can't stay here since we killed him."

"Like hell we can't. I'm not leaving until I know who these other sick fucks are that we're up against."

Leaving without knowing how many people are here would be a wasted trip. One thing I'm doing is making sure my friends stay safe. I have a duty to protect them. It's one of the reasons I came here. I refuse to leave until I can find out more about these people. Chances are they are like this man. We've got to take them out before they're able to get to us.

CHAPTER 19
JOEY

I HAND Isabella a bottle of water, and she gulps down nearly half of it. "How did you get here without them noticing you?"

Isabella shakes her head. "I hid out by Daddy's old barn when they came. Some of them stayed the night at the house. When they left, I took off running through the woods so I could come here."

To think Sunny and Timmy went out doesn't sit well with me. "You can't go back out there. You've got to stay here with us now."

Isabella sits down on the couch, and tears stream down her face. "There were ten of them, and I had to watch them kill all of my family. One by one, they slit all their necks."

Ava's eyes get wide, and she shakes her head. "I'm so sorry you had to experience something horrific."

I wrap my arms around her as sobs escape from her lips. I'm angry with myself for allowing this to happen. If I would have went there last night, I could have stopped this from happening. Several seconds pass, and after she's no longer crying is when I speak. "Have you ever seen those people before?" I ask.

I'm trying to get a handle on where those people came from.

Isabella sniffs. "We went to go get our box the day before yesterday. Those people were on top of the building and wouldn't let us get anything. Daddy told them off before we left. I guess one of them followed us out of town when we went searching for food."

I don't understand why Henry didn't come here and mention it to me. Maybe he got busy and had other things that needed to be done. The two of us would talk every week to check on one another. Seeing we have always been in such proximity with being neighbors.

Landon comes out of his bedroom and joins us in the living room. "I heard what you told my dad. You're more than welcome to sleep in my room."

Isabella stares down at her hands and then looks at us again. Her hazel eyes are puffy from crying so much. "I'm not going to be sleeping in anyone's room. I was scratched in the back by a zombie this morning. I just came here to warn you."

I lift up the back of her shirt to see if what she says is true. There's two deep claw marks on her back.

Landon's eyes go wide. "You survived monstrous human beings but not a zombie. This shit is so fucked up."

I put her shirt back down, speechless. I've known her for the past year. She's only eighteen. It's much too young to die. She's got her entire life ahead.

I get up from the couch, unable to sit in here another minute. I've got to go outside and clear my head. I'm about to fucking blow.

I open up the door and sit down on the porch steps. The inferno burning inside me erupts. These fuckers who did this to my friends are going to pay. They don't get to live on this earth anymore. Even if I have to kill every last one of them myself.

The door opens, and I look up at Ava. Her eyebrows draw

together, and she comes over to sit down beside me. "I'm sorry about your friends. I know how difficult it is to lose the ones we love the most."

My anger simmers down at her words. To me it means everything she came out here to talk to me. "I wish things didn't come down to this. She is just a teenager and is supposed to live longer than this. I should've been there when they came to that house."

She puts her hand on my cheek, and I tilt my head to the side. "You're wrong about that. Think about what could have happened to Landon. She said there's ten of them, and you would have never been able to fight them off yourself."

I grab ahold of her hand and put my fingers through hers. "When I retired from the army, I bought this farm. Many people didn't like me around these parts. I was an outsider. Henry and his family welcomed me here with open arms. Helped me tend to my garden and even fed us every weekend."

I sure am going to miss him. I wish things wouldn't have come to this.

"He seems like he was a good man."

"A better man than I could ever be."

There will never be another person like him. A man who had a way of always lifting my spirits.

The vein stands out in Landon's neck, and his hands shake. "Come quick! Isabella's burning up!"

I hurry inside the house, and Isabella's lying down on the couch. Sweat drips down her forehead, and her skin is flushed. This can't be good. She's probably getting ready to turn. "Landon, you and Ava aren't going to want to see this."

"You're right. I don't." Landon walks down the hall and disappears out of sight.

Ava shakes her head. "I'm not going anywhere."

Isabella closes her eyes. "You need to do it now. I don't want anything to happen to any of you because of me. Daddy and the rest of my family are going to be waiting on the other side. Go ahead and do it. I'm at peace."

I grab the pillow that's sitting on the other end of the couch and press it against her head. My finger stops before I pull the trigger. This day is going to stick with me for the rest of my life. She's the first person I've ever had to end like this. Killing someone as innocent as her isn't something I signed up for. This will never settle right with me.

She's going to come back as a zombie. Pull the trigger and do it now!

"I'm sorry," I say.

I press my finger down on the trigger, and the bullet rips through the pillow. Blood washes over the pillow, and it falls from my hands. There's a hole in Isabella's head, and it went clean through.

You're the one who ended her life. No one else did.

My chest goes numb, and the room spins around me. I try to think clearly, but my mind races, and I can't think straight. I fold an arm across my stomach and wish this world was different. It would make things more bearable to live.

A small hand wraps around my waist, and I focus on Ava, who's right beside me. "Let's go outside and sit down," she suggests.

I go out the door, wanting to escape the reality of this. The sun's rays nearly blind me, jolting me to my senses. "You shouldn't have stayed and witnessed that," I say.

Her lips turn down in a frown. "I wished someone would have been there with me when I had to..." She doesn't finish the sentence, her voice trailing off.

I wrap my arm around her, and she cradles her head against my shoulder. "You don't have to worry about that anymore. I'll be the one doing it from here on out," I reply.

I'm not leaving her to do something so horrifying. It wouldn't be right when I'm the one better equipped to handle this.

Heather and Brooke come walking towards the house.

I've got to warn the two of them about Isabella. She meant something to the two of them. It's not like she was a stranger, since they lived here on the farm before the divorce. "Isabella's dead. She's in the living room."

Brooke's lip trembles, and she clenches her fist. "She was one of my best friends. I can't believe she's gone."

Heather wrinkles her brows and bites her lip. "What about Henry and everyone else?"

"They're all dead. People came to their house and killed them," I say.

Tears stream down Heather's face. "Brooke, let's go outside and take a nap. I don't feel so well."

"The two of you need to be careful," I warn.

Neither one of them say anything to me before going in the door. I hope they keep what I said in mind. Things may not be the best between all of us, but I'm not so sure I would ever be able to live with myself if anything happened to them.

IT'S the first time since I've been here Brooke and Heather haven't acted hostile towards me. Hopefully this is something I can grow accustomed to. The tension between them isn't something I can stand. We've all endured a lot today already. Things just need to be peaceful.

Joey gives my thigh a squeeze before standing up from the porch steps. "I wasn't thinking clearly with Isabella. Now the couch is ruined, and no one will be able to sleep on it."

You did the right thing. It's just a couch. Don't beat yourself up over it.

"She was a threat to all of us, and you did what you needed to protect us," I say.

Joey holds out his hand to help me up. Sparks ignite the flames that are growing around my heart. "You're right about that. I just wish I didn't have to. It's a tough blow to us all," Joey replies.

The toughest blow is knowing Timmy and Sunny are out there. There are ten of them, so that means they are outnumbered. My stomach is in knots, knowing very well they might not be coming back alive. The reality of that is more apparent now than ever.

"Was Sunny in the military too?" I ask.

Joey stalks into the house, and I'm right beside him. "The two of us were stationed together in Iraq."

It does ease my mind a little but not a lot. A lump forms in my throat, and I try to push all the bad thoughts out of my head. I try not to think the worst, but it's hard not to. The only comfort is knowing Sunny is equipped to deal with this situation since he's a military man.

Landon's in the kitchen when we walk into the house. He comes over to Joey and gives him a hug. "We should dig her a grave. It's something she deserves."

Joey nods. "I don't want you out there without me. I've got to clean up this mess I made first."

I divert my gaze away from Isabella's body. It reminds me so much of Angel and the way I had to take his life. My arms drop down to my sides, and a lump forms in my throat. Tears threaten to roll down my face, but I press them back. "I'll help in any way I can. Just tell me what you need me to do."

Joey squeezes my shoulder, and it gives me comfort. "I'm going to throw this damn couch outside. There's no use keeping it anymore. I've got plenty more blankets and pillows upstairs in the closet."

So that's settled then. I'll help him carry the couch outside. It's all just a matter of him carrying her body.

My mouth is dry, and I stroll into the kitchen to get a bottle of water. The case of water is sitting on the floor beside the fridge. There are only ten bottles, and that's alarming to me. We're probably going to have to boil water from the river soon.

I open up the bottle of water and take a drink. It does everything in the world to soothe my parched throat.

Landon comes over and sits beside me. "I'm glad my dad has you to talk to about things."

Talking to him has helped keep me sane.

"I know a little bit about your dad but don't know anything about you."

If Joey and I are going to end up being a thing, I want to know about Landon. I refuse to let things be awkward between the two of us. He's his son and the most important part of his life.

Landon's knee bounces up and down beside me. "What do you want to know about me?"

I blink, and my pulse quickens. "Has Joey always been a hard-ass father?" I ask.

Landon laughs, and it breaks the ice between us. "Dad's only been a hard ass since the end of the world happened."

"And he's got a reason to be," I answer.

The vein in Landon's neck pulses, and he cracks his knuckles. "The thing that's bothered me the most is not knowing who my real mom is. It bothers me to no end that she didn't want me when I was born."

My throat tightens at what he's gone through. It just confirms my suspicions about Heather not being his real mother. "That's her loss since she's missed out on knowing such a good person. You lucked out with having a good father."

Landon's face softens, and he gives me a small smile. "Heather has been with me ever since I was a little boy. I'm grateful to have her too."

I dislike Heather for being so hostile towards me. At the same time, I've got to understand where Landon's coming from. I'll try my hardest to get along with her and Brooke for everyone's sake. It will make things easier if I try to keep the peace.

I squeeze Landon's leg. "You're lucky to have the two of them in your life."

The door opens, and Joey carries Isabella outside.

Landon stands up. "Will you help me move the couch?"

I nod. "I'll grab the end closest to the door."

Landon goes to the back end of the couch. "So do you think you and my old man will be a thing?"

I'm fully aware of the blood and brains on the pillow. I look away from it and concentrate on what we need to be doing.

I lift up the couch, and Landon does too. "I like him and want to get to know more about him. It's too early to tell how far things will escalate between the two of us."

I get a good grip on the couch, and I lead the way outdoors with it.

Landon comes out behind me, and then we set it down. "If the two of you end up being a thing, you have my approval."

I grin. "Thank you, that's nice to know."

Joey is at the bottom of the winding driveway near the garden. Sweat drips down from his forehead, and he takes off his shirt. A shovel is in his hand, and he's busy digging Isabella's grave.

My face grows hot as I stare at his perfectly toned abs. I want to run my hands across his delicious body and take away his pain of having lost his friend. Joey catches me staring at him and looks up at me. His lips turn up in a grin.

Landon strolls down the steps to join him. "We need to say a few words about Isabella after we put her into the ground."

I fold my arms across my chest and saunter towards the two of them. "When I was a teenager, I used to spend most of my summers here with Angel. We would go down the ravine to fish and swim in the river."

A lump forms in my throat as I think about Angel. He was the best friend a girl could ever ask for. The hardest thing is knowing that he's gone. I think about how I stayed with him yesterday until he took his last breath. I'll never want to remember him like that.

Joey stops shoveling and wraps an arm around my waist.

"I take it that's the reason you wanted to come here to the farm."

"It's the only place I knew where to go." My voice is barely above a whisper.

Landon picks up the shovel and digs up dirt. "Being here with all of us is a good place to be."

CHAPTER 21
SUNNY

I'M ready for those other fuckers to come. I've got to take them down so we can live at the farm in peace. I already killed one son of a bitch, and I'm eager to kill more. I lean forward and clutch my hands together. Now it's just a waiting game.

Timmy clasps his knees together and grips the kitchen chair. "We don't know what we're up against."

I shrug. "Do you think I don't realize that? Look, I'm not leaving here until this entire group is dead. You saw how that man was going to feed that zombie. The rest of these people are just like him. If they weren't, they wouldn't be here."

His hand shakes, and he falls to the floor. "I don't want to die. I've got a sister in Grayback. I've still got family left in this world. These people are going to come in here and kill us."

I bite the inside of my cheek. "Listen, no one asked you to come here. I'm not begging you to stay. There's the door, and you can go out it any time."

I don't give a fuck if I sound harsh. This guy doesn't mean shit to me. He sure as hell isn't going to get in the way of what I came here to do. It's pathetic if you ask me, and he needs to grow a pair of balls.

He scratches his head and stands up straight. "I'm not leaving this place without you."

A van pulls into the driveway, and I duck down beside the fridge. I dart my gaze to the window, and my stomach churns. I'm ready to get up and spring into action. Now is the time to finally see who I'm going to be up against. "Get over here where I'm at," I hiss.

He crawls over to where I'm at. He balls up his fist at his side. "What are we going to do?" His voice cracks.

I watch as a woman gets out of the driver's side of the van. A man gets out of the passenger side. My lips turn up into a smile, and every cell in my body vibrates. This is going to be easy taking them down. Adrenaline washes over my body, and the demons I've had stored away are about to be let out. I'm so pumped and ready to do this once they get inside this house.

The middle door slides open, and seven people come filing out.

Fuck. There's too many of them. I don't have nearly enough bullets to take them out.

I rub my hands against my pant leg. "We're going out the back door."

Timmy gets up from his position on the floor and moves towards the exit. I'm right behind him. The hair on my neck stands up, and I lick my lips.

Here we go.

He opens up the door and takes off running. The screen door slams behind me, and I run close behind him. My breath catches in my chest, and I keep going. This isn't going to be the end of me. These mother fuckers aren't going to take me hostage or kill me. Forget that shit.

Gunshots echo through the mountain as we go down the hill. "You two aren't going to get far!" a voice close behind us calls out.

I tilt my head to the side and glance back. Two men with

athletic builds are gaining on us. We've got to push harder, or they're going to catch us.

Timmy stumbles over a rock, and bones crunch. He screams out in agony and grabs ahold of his broken foot. "Help me, Sunny! Don't let me die out here!"

I think about it for a brief second. He can't walk on that foot now. If I stop to help him, it will slow me down. There's no way I'm going to let some guy I just met end my life along with his. "I'm sorry, but I can't."

Timmy grips my pants. "Please don't leave me here. I'm begging you."

I pry his hands off me. "It was nice meeting you."

I'm sorry I have to do this. The two of us had a good chat.

I don't wait for Timmy's response. The adrenaline pumps through my veins when I take off running. I pass by trees, and the sun's shining down on me. Sweat drips off my forehead, and there's a pounding in my head.

"Please don't hurt me!" Timmy yells.

I can't turn back around. I had to make a choice to save myself.

"I didn't do anything to any of you!" Timmy yells.

"You were in the wrong place at the wrong time," one of the men says.

The gunshot blast cuts through the woods. I'm certain he's dead.

I make my way farther into the forest and finally catch sight of the road. A car goes by, and I duck behind a tree to remain out of sight. Growls escape from the ground below me. A zombie with no legs crawls towards me. I take my pocket knife out of my pants and stick it in its head. The growls are no more.

Footsteps crunch in the woods behind me, and I edge my way towards the road. It's only just a couple of minutes until I get to the farm. Then I can send these psychos straight to hell where they belong.

My feet hit the gravel, and I run as fast as I can. I gain speed with each passing second, and my legs are like Jell-O. The house is within my reach. I've just got to go a little farther.

You can do this. Don't let these crazy son of a bitches win.

Joey's standing outside on the porch when I round the corner. He's got nothing but concern for me on his face. "We heard gunshots. Are you okay?" Joey asks.

I bend over so that I can catch my breath. "There's people following me. They're coming."

Joey gets his gun ready to fire. "We've got to go inside."

I step inside the house. Landon, Ava, Brooke, and Heather are all gathered around the kitchen.

"Timmy's dead."

He's fucking dead. It was either me or him.

Heather lets out a gasp, and her eyes go wide. "How did that happen?"

"Things got tough going down that mountain," I say.

Landon bares his teeth. "At least we gave him a chance by coming here."

It's just too damn bad he broke his foot.

Brooke folds an arm across her stomach. "You did, and that's more than enough."

Ava's lips turn down in a frown. "It must have been horrible what happened."

Wasn't the greatest thing that ever was, but I survived.

Joey's got an unreadable expression on his face. "I'm just glad you're back in one piece."

Not only could I have been bit or scratched by that zombie. Crazy mother fuckers are after me too. It's good to be alive and breathing.

Several seconds pass by, and I don't think the fuckers are going to come. There's always the possibility of them going back home to get reinforcements.

Landon's gaze is glued to the window. "Dad, we've got company coming!" A terrified urgency strangles his words.

"Everybody get down on the floor! Me and Sunny have got this handled!" Joey demands.

The same man from earlier gets out of the car. He's got a gun in his hands, but no one else is with him. "Joey, we've got to get a clear shot," I say.

The man knocks on the door, and Joey hides behind it. "You killed my best friend, and I know you're in there!"

Joey's breathing is rapid. "Open the door, and I'll catch him off guard."

I edge my way closer to the entryway, and my chest tingles. This guy could try anything before he sets foot inside. Only somebody stupid would walk into a trap. My hand flies to my gun in my pants. Nobody's going to die today except for this fucker. I'm going to make sure of it.

Joey gets out his gun. "I'm ready," he mouths towards me.

My stomach churns when my hand is on the door handle. We're not going to let this guy come in here unleashing bullets. We've got to take him the fuck down.

The door opens, and Joey comes up closer to me. He doesn't give the man a chance to put his finger on the trigger. Bullets riddle the man's body, and there's a fiery rage in Joey's eyes. This isn't a side of him I've seen since Iraq.

Screams erupt from all three of the women. They've probably never seen Joey kill anyone before. They better get used to it since this will probably happen again. There's other people out there. Ones we haven't done away with yet.

Joey lets out a sigh of relief. "Isabella said there were ten of them up there."

"That's way too fucking many if you ask me," I answer.

Ava gets up from her position. When she sees the man and puddle of blood, she wrinkles her nose. "I'm going upstairs. I feel safer up there."

"I'm going with you," Landon replies.

Makes perfect sense. If any more of them come, they'll probably be coming through the first floor first. Hell, there's doors and windows. Will be easier to access.

Heather and Brooke both disappear into their bedroom.

Landon and Ava both go up the stairs, leaving me and Joey all alone. I've got to tell him about what happened with Timmy. "Do you mind if we step outside?"

Joey gets up from the floor and leads the way to the outdoors. "Sure."

I sit down on the steps and light a cigarette. The scary thing about what happened is I don't feel anything. I'm not sad or upset about him dying. It makes me believe I'm sort of a monster or psycho even. "It's my fault Timmy died. He fell, and I didn't help him."

Joey shrugs. "I can't say I blame you. I would've done the exact same thing."

SUNNY HELPS me drag the body outside. I'm not quite sure what I want to do with it. Getting him out of my house is the first step. Now I've got to clean up this bloody mess. I wasn't thinking clearly when I shot him. It would've been easier just to strangle him to death but a lot more personable.

This takes me back to the days I was in the army. Not a good thing to think about, considering I killed people back then. The people I did kill had to be killed, or my fellow soldiers would have become victims. It sucks because I had to kill a woman who was holding a grenade. It was one of the biggest things that led to my drinking.

Landon hands me some towels from the bathroom. "Have we got any bleach?"

I shake my head. "I'm not sure. We've got other disinfectants upstairs."

He hurries off to get me what I need.

I glance out the window and see Sunny walk down to the camper. He might be thinking about what happened with Timmy. He shouldn't beat himself up over it because it's not worth it, though it will weigh on his conscience some. Unless he's to the point of shutting his humanity off. I hope that I would know it if he was at that point.

He comes down the stairs with a spray bottle. "There's no more left after this."

I take the bottle from his hands and spray the blood. "You know I had to do this, right?" I ask.

I don't want my son to be scared of me.

He sits with his back pressed against the wall. "Anybody can see this man wanted us dead. Wouldn't have wanted him to end any of us. You did the right thing regardless of what anyone has to say."

I am going to let Ava be alone for a while. I don't want her to think of me as some kind of monster. I am a man who has a soul and a heart. It wasn't necessarily easy for me to pull the trigger when it came to him or Isabella earlier. I just try not to let it eat away at my soul. I did what I had to so we could all survive.

"I would like to tell you this isn't something you'll ever have to do. If I did that, I would be lying," I say.

A frown forms on his face. "Maybe there will come a point in time when we'll have law and order."

Anything is possible, but it's probably going to be something far into the future.

There's been something weighing on my mind. Something I've been dying to ask him. "I like living here on the farm. It's been our home for the last year. But there's probably more out there. Would you ever want to leave?"

He thinks about it for a minute. "I don't want to leave this place unless we have to. The thought of being out there not knowing what to expect scares me."

I understand his concern and agree. Being out there would mean living in hardship.I spray the blood with the bleach and then wipe it down with the towels. "There may come a point in time when we do have to leave. I just hope that time doesn't come any time soon."

He nods. "It would be nice to know who's good people. That's what scares me the most when it comes to leaving.

We've already experienced crazy ones. Makes me believe everybody good is dead."

I wipe up the rest of the blood and guts. "All the good people are probably in hiding. I'm sure they've probably experienced the crazies like we have. We've just got to find them."

Brooke walks into the living room. "I've got to go pee and want you to come with me, Landon."

Despite me and Heather now being divorced, the two of them are still close. They grew up together, so it would sadden me if they weren't.

"You two don't be out there too long," I say.

There's other people still out there, and we don't know if they're going to come here or not. Hanging around outside isn't such a good idea. Not when we're in the situation we're in now.

"We won't, old man," Landon replies before going out the door.

Brooke rolls her eyes but doesn't say anything to me.

I put the dirty towels in the trash can in the kitchen. Then go to the window to watch Brooke and Landon. The two of them are alright. There's no doubt in my mind they'll come back inside as soon as Brooke's finished. Now it's time to check on Ava.

I make my way up the stairs and knock on the bedroom door. "I'm coming in," I warn.

Ava's gaze goes to my chest, and I have an aching desire for her to touch me. Laying her against the bed and fucking her senseless would make this day so much better.

"I take it you didn't have time to freshen up."

I go over to the mirror and stare at my reflection. Blood is caked on my bare chest. Washing up will be something I do after the two of us get finished talking. There's baby wipes in the cabinet downstairs, and they'll do the trick.

I sit down on the bed and close my eyes. "I had to come check on you first to see how you were doing."

She rubs her fingers against mine, and it turns me on. My erection throbs against me, and I open up my eyes. It would be nice if we could stay here like this for the next couple of hours. I'm the most comfortable I've been all day.

"I'm doing just fine now that you're here with me," she says.

I laugh. "I wish I could stay for longer than a couple of minutes. I've still got to take that trash out before this house smells to high heavens. That wouldn't be a good thing."

She grins. "No, it wouldn't be a good thing. Then we'd all be going down to the camper."

Heat radiates through my chest. "Sunny wouldn't like that one bit. He's claimed that camper as his own."

"That camper wasn't here when I was a teenager. A trampoline was there in its place." Her voice cracks.

I want more than anything to wrap an arm around her. If I wasn't so damn filthy, I would.

"What was it like being here back then?" I ask.

Her lip trembles. "It was the one time in my life I've been at peace. I didn't have a worry in the world when I was here. Then when I would go back home, reality set in. The reality being I was an unwanted daughter."

I clench my fist at my side as the anger surges through my veins. Nobody should ever be made to feel this way. It infuriates me her own parents would do this to her. "You shouldn't let your parents get you down. It was their loss for not playing a part in your life."

A tear streams down her face, and she wipes it away with her hand. "I've tried not to for the longest time. I think about them now more than ever. I wonder if they're still alive so I can give them a piece of my mind."

Fuck it. She needs me to give her comfort. I can't sit here and do absolutely nothing. It doesn't matter that I'm filthy.

I wrap an arm around her shoulders, and she scoots closer to me. Her head goes to the crook of my neck. A waterfall of tears streams down her face. Now's the time for her to let everything out. I don't plan on going anywhere.

"Landon's mother wanted to get an abortion with him. She was seventeen when we got pregnant with him and was still in high school. I begged her not to. She reluctantly had him and gave him to me. He's been with me ever since then."

She shakes her head. "I would have done anything to have been able to carry a child."

I wrinkle my nose and stroke my throat, thinking about her. It makes me absolutely sick. "The sad thing about it is, she got married about five years ago. Has three other kids and wouldn't bother to call Landon."

She lets out a sigh and glances up at me. "I didn't get my tubes tied. I just quit trying to make babies. It wasn't worth being happy and then giving up my hopes with miscarrying."

My eyes narrow and focus on her. I squeeze the inside of her thigh, and she stares intently at me. "We should practice making a baby," I say.

Her cheeks turn rosy red, and she giggles. "I'm not opposed to that at the right time. As long as you have some condoms."

I rub my hand across her cheekbone, and she melts against my touch. It's so tempting to take her right here. "I'll get some condoms the next time I go on a run."

She licks her lips, and my insides go wild. I don't know if she realizes how crazy she's making me.

"I've not laid with a man ever since my divorce. I was just never interested in doing it with anyone until I met you."

It's a damn shame she didn't let herself have any fun. The two of us are going to be having fun alright. We're going to get down and dirty. My stress needs to be lifted from me.

"It's been a year for me. Even then, that woman wasn't as pretty as you. She didn't have long blonde hair or a drop-dead gorgeous smile. Or a sexy body full of curves like you do."

Her entire face lights up the room. "My blonde hair is getting some gray since I can't go to a hairstylist anymore."

I reach out and take the hair bow out of her hair. There's a few gray strands around her face but not many. "I love your hair. It's just a sign of you getting older."

She laughs. "I beg to differ. It would be nice to be blonde-headed forever."

I'm going to find her some blonde hair dye when I go out on a run. It will do everything in the world to make her happy. Her smile will make my world go around.

There's an abrupt knock on the door. "Dad, can I talk to you?" Landon asks.

"Sure, come on in," I answer.

Ava pulls apart from me and leans against the headboard. She closes her eyes. I suspect to pretend to not listen to anything going on.

Landon focuses on me, and I can tell something's wrong. "I was wondering if you could stay in my room with me tonight."

After everything that's happened today, I couldn't imagine doing anything else. Sunny will have to take watch by himself for awhile. I'll head outside once Landon gets some shut eye. Things are much too dangerous now for me to sleep in his room.

"I wouldn't want to be anywhere else other than with you," I say.

He lets out a sigh of relief. "Today's just put a lot of things in perspective for me."

"You'll always have a place in my bedroom beside me. No matter how old you get," I reply.

"I guess I'm just afraid of the boogeyman," he jokes.

If I was his age and had my whole life ahead, I would be too.

CHAPTER 23
SUNNY

I'M FUCKING STARVING, but now isn't the time to start a fire. It will only be a way for people to recognize us. I'm not scared of anyone. Hell, I've killed people before. I just don't want to put the people here at risk. Joey's my friend and battle buddy. I wouldn't want anything to happen to him or his family. Even if his ex-wife and former stepdaughter get on my damn nerves.

I dig through the box of food in the kitchen. There's some spaghetti, pasta sauce, and cans of soup. None of those things seem appealing to me without warming up. I wish those people would get here if they're coming. Waiting on them isn't something I'm thrilled about.

Landon's sitting at the kitchen table with a bottle of water in his hand. "You have got the same idea I do."

I sit down beside him. "Would be nice to go hunting. We'd have meat to eat for a while."

He takes a swig of water. "Deer meat sounds great right about now."

He's right. It would be amazing. I'm a meat-eater kind of guy, not some vegetarian. It blows. Would be nice to head to the grocery store and buy some hamburger meat. It would keep me full longer than eating what we have here. Not that I'm complaining.

"I'm going to catch us something good before this week's out."

Hopefully we'll kill those fucking people, and it will be safer to go back out.

He raises his eyebrows. "That's something to look forward to."

"Yeah, it really is."

Shit. I used to go hunting all the time when my wife was still alive. To me it was fun escaping into the woods for a little while. A good place to relax and let the rest of the world fade away.

I quit going after she died since I had my little boy to raise. It never felt right leaving him for a couple of hours for my own benefit.

His belly growls. "Starving is worse than being in hell," he grumbles.

I don't have a comment to that, so I keep my mouth shut. There's a pounding in my head about to drive me insane. A cigarette's just the thing I need. It will do everything in the world to soothe my soul. Going outside to smoke seems tempting.

Joey gets baby wipes from the cabinet. "I'll get supper started once I freshen up."

Landon parts his lips and flops back into the chair. "That's music to my ears."

A scream from the downstairs bedroom grabs my attention. I jump up and draw my gun in front of me. I'm not sure whether it was Brooke or Heather who screamed.

Joey takes one look at Landon. "Go upstairs and stay with Ava. Don't move until I tell you to get out."

Landon moves towards the stairs, and something catches my eye. There's a man outside the window staring back at us.

He's got a smirk on his face and looks like the devil himself. "Dad, do you fucking see that?" Landon demands.

"Stay away from the windows. We don't know what this fucker will try to do," Joey says.

Landon crawls into the middle of the living room. "That was the man we saw yesterday. I couldn't forget his face even if I tried."

Ava appears at the top of the stairs. "What's going on?"

"Stay there and shut the door behind you! People are trying to fucking get in!" Joey yells.

Another scream comes out of the bedroom downstairs. I hurry to see what those bitches are so afraid of.

Heather and Brooke are both sitting on the floor. They've got their arms wrapped around each other, giving each other comfort.

Heather looks up at me and points to the window. "A woman was looking in. She had a hammer in her hand. Oh God, Sunny, she's going to get in here and try to kill all of us." Her lip trembles when she speaks.

There's no one dying on my watch except for the fuckers outside. I'll kill every single one of them with my bare hands even if I have to. What they're trying to do by creeping in the windows is scare us. I've got news for them. They piss me the fuck off. I'll never be afraid of them.

The glass shatters from another room downstairs. The woman must have seen me come in here.

I have my gun trained in front of me when I leave the bedroom. I'm more than ready to kill. Rage takes over my body at all of the shit I've had to do in this lifetime. Things that not just anyone would be able to do. Maybe one day I'll have remorse, but that day isn't today.

I shut the door behind me and walk into the hallway. My heart hammers out of my chest, and I'm on high alert. The last thing I want is for that woman to come at me out of nowhere. I'm not going to let her hit me with that hammer.

The first room I come to is the bathroom, and the door's shut. I carefully open the door and step into the room. Glass is scattered all over the bathroom floor. This is the room that this crazy psychotic bitch entered. She's still in here somewhere. I've got to find her before she sneaks up on me. A sour taste forms in my mouth, and I focus on my surroundings. There's a toilet seat sitting in the corner and a sink sitting beside it. My first thoughts are of her being in the bathtub. It just seems like an obvious place for her to be.

I edge my way to the bathtub and clench my teeth. My skin prickles, and I hesitate before pulling back the shower curtain. This seems way too obvious for her to be.

Here goes nothing.

A shiver runs up and down my spine as I pull back the shower curtain. Fuck. Nobody's in the bathtub. I hold in my breath and listen closely to the footsteps walking across the floor behind me.

I spin around just as she charges towards me with the hammer. The hammer's above her head, and I dodge to miss it. She takes another swing at me. I lower my head into her stomach and tackle her to the floor. The gun and hammer scatter across the floor out of reach.

A smirk appears on her psychotic, deranged face. "The two of us came here because we just wanted to play a game."

Fucking psychotic bitch.

"You're not playing any more games with innocent people," I say.

Die, you fucking bitch.

I place my hands around her neck, and she claws at my arms. She kicks her feet underneath me, and I tighten my grip around her throat. There's no way in hell she's going to break free.

My little boy crosses my mind, and the rage ignites the demons living inside of me. I squeeze her throat harder. Bones crunch, and her arms stop flapping. I watch the life escape from her eyes and then back up away from her.

I grab the hammer and smash her head in. It wouldn't be wise not to. She'll come back as a zombie. None of us need to be ripped apart by some flesh-eating piece of shit.

A gunshot rips through the air, followed by shattered glass. I make my way back into the living room to see what the hell's going on. Landon's mouth is open, and Joey cracks his neck. The man who was spying on us is lying on the porch steps.

"That must have been one hell of a fucking shot," I say.

Joey hadn't even given the man a chance to get inside.

"Nobody's getting in my house and killing the people most precious to me," Joey replies.

Now we've got to worry about getting rid of the bodies. I'm hungry and ready to fucking eat.

CHAPTER 24
AVA

I GET up from the bed and walk out the door. It's impossible to sit up here after hearing that gunshot thirty minutes ago. I've stayed glued to the bed the entire time until I finally muster the courage to get up.

Joey's standing on the steps, and he's got an unreadable expression on his face. "Sunny's fixing us all spaghetti for supper."

Food sounds amazing right about now. That soup from earlier is starting to wear off.

I clear my throat. "How many people were here?" I ask.

"Two, but you don't have to worry about any of them."

I couldn't be more grateful the problem is taken care of for now. It does still trouble me that others are still out there.

The disinfectant is strong as we pass by the window. I take a step back and stare at the broken glass in disbelief. Only one gunshot was fired, and it must have been a good hit.

I part my lips and wonder what's going to happen next. "What are we going to do about those other people at the house?"

The two of us step outside, and I scrunch my nose. There are three dead bodies piled up near the door. I would've hoped they had cleaned this up before now. Maybe Joey was eager to see me.

"Right now we're not going to do anything about them. They could be waiting on us to come up there. We're going to stay here for now and talk about our next course of action."

What he's saying makes sense. I don't think there would be any use us going up there now. Timmy already died at their hands, and we still don't know for sure how many of them there are going to be. Isabella said there were ten of them there. That number could always change. My hair rises up on the back of my neck, just thinking about more of them. I quickly push those thoughts away. If I think about it while I'm trying to eat, I'll become nauseous.

Landon's got a bowl of food in his hands. "This did the trick, old man."

Joey grins. "You're never going to go hungry. I'm going to make sure of it."

Sunny hands me a plate of food and a fork. "It's hot, so be careful."

The steam is coming out of the top, and I blow on it. "Thank you for the warning."

I don't care if the spaghetti burns my tongue. I just want to get my belly full. I'm not going to wait until it's completely cooled down to eat.

Joey puts his hand on the center of my back. "Let's go sit down so we all can talk."

Heather and Brooke are both sitting in the garage. The two of them look up at me and Joey. Brooke glares at me, and Heather rolls her eyes. So much for the two of them being nice to me.

Don't let them get to you. It's been a long day for everyone.

I sit down at the picnic table away from them. "Are you not going to eat anything?"

Joey nods. "I'm going to wait until everyone has had their share of what they want."

His hospitality makes my admiration for him grow. He's got to be hungry.

I take a bite of the spaghetti, and it burns the inside of my mouth. It's absolutely delicious, and I could eat another plate. I'm not going to because I don't want to be greedy. "I've been thinking I could clean your house tomorrow."

I can't just sit in his house all day and not do anything. I'll go stir crazy.

Joey squeezes my leg, and butterflies form in my stomach. "I'll get you some cleaner together when we go back up to the house."

Landon has a seat beside Joey. "Now I can actually think since I've got something to eat."

"We're going on a run either tomorrow or the next day." Joey stands up and goes to the front of the garage.

Sunny's standing outside with a cigarette in his mouth. "I'm going to stay out here and keep a watch on the house."

Makes sense even though they could come in from the other side. My heart races, and pain forms in my chest. I let out a deep breath. There's no reason to get worked up about this. Joey and Sunny will make sure no one's in the house when we get done here.

Joey paces around the garage and stops to crack his knuckles. "I do realize there's more people up there in the house. It would be unwise for us to keep going up there. We don't have any idea of what they're planning."

I finish off the rest of my spaghetti and immediately wish I had a water. I'll have to get one once I go back inside.

Sunny's eyes go black. "We've got to do something about them. It's unwise for us to just sit here. We'll become an easy target to all of them. These people are sick. They had a fucking zombie tied up against the wall."

Nausea takes over, and throw-up forms in my mouth. I swallow down the vomit and get ahold of myself. These people are sicker than what I imagined them to be.

Joey clenches his fists at his side. "I'm not letting you or anyone else go back up there. Timmy's dead, and no one else is dying because of these maniacs. You're one of my friends, and I can't let you put yourself at risk for all of us."

I don't want to see anyone else get hurt. We've just got to be prepared if something else were to happen. The harsh reality is more things could happen knowing our enemy is so close. I say they're our enemy, cause if they weren't, today wouldn't have went like it was. Timmy wouldn't be dead, and those people wouldn't have come down here.

Sunny takes a puff off his cigarette and blows out smoke. "Whatever we do, we all better be loaded. Those fuckers could come at us at any time. I'm telling you right now, not one of them could be good."

Heather pinches her throat and then rubs her cheekbones. "What exactly did you see when you went to the house earlier today?"

I'm not so sure I want to hear Sunny's reply. I brace myself for what he's going to say.

Sunny rolls his eyes. "I saw a dead woman in a bathtub. Her throat was slit, and those fuckers were going to feed that woman to the zombie. My opinion is that's what they do to people they kill."

Brooke runs out of the garage, bends over, and throws up all over the grass. "You should've just kept that to yourself."

Sunny smirks. "Heather wanted to know, so I told her."

Joey stands in between the two of them. "Now's not the time for this nonsense. We don't know much about this group. There could be others out there we didn't see. More than what we originally thought."

The veins pop out of Landon's neck. "There might come a time when we have to leave the farm after all."

The thought of being out there in the world will never settle with me. Hopefully if a God does exist, we won't have to any time soon. This group might just let us go. It's not like we've got any quarrel with them. Or at least I don't think we do.

Joey shakes his head. "We're not letting these people drive us out of here. We've got to fight back and be strong. This place is my home, and I'm not leaving so freely."

Brooke flares her nostrils and pulls out strands of her hair. "It might be your home, but it will never be mine. My home is with Matt, in case you've fucking forgotten about that! I'll go back out there and find him. You're not going to stop me!"

Heather wraps her arms around Brooke. "If the farm falls, we won't defend it. We would leave and fend for ourselves."

I watch the two of them walk away from all of us. They're going out by the barn, which is about fifty feet away from us. It's not good for them to be so far away from us, but I sure as hell am not going after them.

"Where are you two going? We're not finished here!" Joey barks after them.

Brooke turns back around and glares at him. "Go ahead and try to stop us."

Joey runs his fingers through his hair and clenches his teeth. He turns to Landon. "What do you say about saying a few words about Isabella?"

Landon hops up from his position and joins Joey. "Sounds like now's as good a time as ever."

Sunny comes over and sits down beside me. "You haven't said a word this entire time. I thought something was wrong."

I blink and then tilt my head to the side. There's one person who I want clarification on, and it's Matt. "Has Brooke always been like this?" I ask.

Sunny laughs. "She's always been a spoiled brat, if that's what you're asking. Matt's been her boyfriend for the past couple of years. He lived in South Carolina before the apocalypse hit. Who knows where the hell he is now."

So that's the reason for her anger and resentment towards Joey. Who knows what happened to him. If it's meant to be between the two of them, they'll find their way back to each other.

I VOLUNTEERED to dig a huge grave for those fuckers we killed. I'm not going to burn their bodies right now. It's getting dark out, and a fire would be a sure sign of making it known people live here. I'm not about to do that when we need to sit down and rest.

Brooke and Heather finally made it up to the house a while ago. Brooke was crying, probably about Matt, and Heather was right by her side. I still don't understand why Joey wanted to bring them here. It's something I probably never will.

Footsteps crunch behind me, and I have my gun trained in front of me. Whoever this is has got another thing coming for sneaking up on me like this. My eyes lock onto Joey's, and he throws his hand out in front of him. "Don't shoot me," Joey teases.

I put my gun back in my pocket. "You should know better than to sneak up on me like that."

He's lucky I didn't pull the trigger. I would have if he would've talked a second later.

He raises his eyebrow and pinches his chin. "I just wanted to come out here a second and see how you're doing."

It's nice for him to have concern for me. I'm doing just

fine. Killing those people didn't affect me any. Would kill more of those fuckers if I had to. Deep down I know he's not talking about that. He's talking about my little boy, Nathan.

I grab a body out of the truck bed and put it in the grave. "You of all people should know I'm doing just fine. Nothing fazes me."

He puts a hand on my shoulder. "Tell me what happened to him. You can't leave it bundled up inside."

I jerk away from him as the anger rushes out of me at once. This isn't something I ever want to talk about. It's bullshit at its finest, but it's something that needs to be said. If I don't talk about this now, he's never going to shut the fuck up about it. "My boy died three months ago when this shit started. A drunk driver took him away from me."

A lump forms in my throat, but I can't cry now. The thing I'm itching to do is kill more people. It will do us all some good, killing the rest of the people from that house. I can't do that though since it would be unwise to. Joey was right about what he said earlier. We don't know much about them, and there could be a lot more.

His lips turn down in a frown. "I just thought he had turned into a zombie."

I laugh without humor. "Him turning into a zombie would've been the end of my life."

His death, if that happened, would have been my fault. It would have been up to me to protect him.

He grabs a body out of the truck. "Help me understand. How did you end up here?"

"Took me a while to get into his hospital room. It was heavily guarded on the outside until too many zombies were out there. Then they all scattered, and I could do what I set out to," I say.

I smile on the inside since Damon is no longer alive anymore. Heat radiates through my chest as I think about those zombies eating him alive. It will always sit well with me. Now he won't be able to crash into anyone ever again.

He throws the body into the grave. "At least you were able to get your revenge. I'm sure it makes you feel fucking fantastic."

You're damn right it does. Killing comes so easy to me.

"It would make me feel even more fantastic if I could kill those fucking people. Then we'd be in peace here at the farm," I reply.

He takes a shovel and scoops dirt on the bodies. "I'm sure we're not finished with them yet. For now we're not going to do anything."

Trying to keep the peace is an awful decision. I don't mind going up there myself and snooping around. It would be easy for me to remain hidden and would help us out in the long run. We would have a hell of a lot more to go on.

"Did you come out here to talk about my little boy or those fucking people?" I demand.

I told him what I wanted to of my little boy. Now I just want to be left alone. He's got his own son, Landon, to take care of. There's no reason for him to be out here with me any longer.

He narrows his eyes at me, displeased with my comment. "I came out here to get some boards so we could board up the house. You took off so fast back there I didn't get a chance to talk to you."

It's nice knowing he wasn't trying to be a pain in my ass. Me having my truck is just convenient. We're going to have to do everything in our power to hold on to it.

I stroll through the barn and find what he's talking about. There's a big pile of wood and boards stacked up in the corner. It'll take us a couple of loads to carry it to the truck. Wish Landon was here to help us.

I gather an armful of the wood and then throw it in the

back of the truck. "Why the hell didn't you do this before now?"

It sure as hell isn't like the apocalypse happened overnight. We've been riding this thing out for three months.

He shrugs. "Didn't think things would become so terrible so quickly. I thought it would take at least a year for this to happen, not just a couple of months."

He probably hasn't wanted to accept the fact that there are more crazier people out there than sane. I guess I can't put much blame on him there. Especially since he's got his son to think about.

"You do realize the state prison is only a few minutes away," I say.

He smirks. "And do you realize we're in the middle of nowhere?"

Being out in the middle of nowhere is what makes this place so good. Now if only those fuckers would leave, we'd be having a good time.

"This place is the best place in the world to be," I reply.

He wipes the sweat from his forehead. "I'm thinking about going on a run tomorrow. We could use some supplies."

"I can keep an eye on Ava, Brooke, and Heather while you're gone," I say.

Not that Heather or Brooke will listen to anything I tell them. I'll spend most of my time probably alone or hanging out with Ava. She seems like a cool chick. I touch the cross necklace I've got around my neck. This thing could've been what kept me alive.

He rocks back and forth before clutching onto the shovel. "I'll take Landon with me. The two of us might be gone a while. It might take us the entire day to find a place to get supplies."

I pat him on the arm. "Don't worry. Everything will be just fine."

He shovels up the rest of the dirt over the bodies. "Landon

wanted to stay up there at the house. He's talking to Brooke about what happened earlier."

I roll my eyes. "There's nothing to talk about. She pulled her hair out and acted crazy."

He doesn't say anything for several minutes. "I'm still wondering if I made the right decision by bringing them here."

Right now he doesn't need to hear me complaining about them. "They didn't have to come if that's what you're getting at. I'm sure you didn't put a gun to their head and threaten to kill them."

He thinks about that for a second. "You're right. I didn't."

"There's nothing keeping the two of them here. They can leave at any time."

He shouldn't have any guilt about anything when he's done more for them than a lot of other people would.

CHAPTER 26

JOEY

LANDON IS in the kitchen with Ava when I walk through the door. "Do you need help with that?" Landon asks.

"The best thing you can do is start covering all the windows downstairs," I say.

We might not be able to get through everything before nightfall. I should've been better prepared for this and feel stupid. This place isn't an easy one to find. So I didn't expect everything that's happened here today. I'm an utter and complete idiot. Today was a lesson within itself. There's other people out there close by, and it's not by some coincidence.

Landon hurries over to the cabinet. He pulls out a hammer and some nails. "I'll start in the bathroom and work my way around."

Before anyone set foot in this house, I made sure it was safe. If anyone was in here now, they would've been heard. It's the only reason I'm not worried about him going into the bathroom by himself.

Now's the chance for the two of us to be alone. "Ava, would you like to help me bring some of the wood inside?"

There's dark circles underneath her eyes. I suspect she's going to go to bed soon. "Putting me to work already, I see," she teases.

I grin. "Somebody's got to help me while Sunny keeps watch."

There's a cool breeze outside, and it's nice not to have sweat running down my face. I'm going to take a bath in the river sooner than I'd like to. Probably in the next three days, if I get a chance. The sun's rays ate me alive today, and I can't stand to smell myself for longer than that.

"I sat down and made a list of everything that was in the house to eat. We've got three cans of soup left, a package of spaghetti, and sauce. There's only a handful bottles of water, but we can go down to the river and boil some," Ava tells me.

I'm grateful she did all of that in her downtime. It's one less thing I have to worry about. "I'll see if I can find any jugs of water anywhere so we don't have to resort to that."

Her face glows at the mention. "Would you mind getting me some toiletries while you're out there?"

I pick up a handful of wood and put it in her outstretched arms. "Anything else?"

She walks up the steps to the house carefully. "I can't think of anything at the moment."

I stare at her ass, swaying back and forth as she makes her way into the house. If it was up to me, we would start fucking tonight. We can just forget the condoms for one night.

Sunny's down by the camper with a cigarette in his mouth. "She's the one you should be after."

I flip him off before gathering up another load of wood. "It's none of your fucking business, but I'm after her. So don't think about touching her."

Sunny snickers. "You should know by now I'm not interested in any women. Those days are over."

I roll my eyes since it's nothing but a lie. This world may be different now, but it would be lonely without another person. Even if that other person is just a lover and a friend. "You're even crazier than what I thought you were."

Sunny takes a drag off his cigarette. "It's a damn good thing you don't know what goes through my mind."

I don't even want to know where this is going. It's the reason I go back up the steps and inside. The first thing I do is set the pile of wood on the kitchen floor beside Ava's load. This should probably be enough wood for now.

I'm going to go check on Landon to see what he's been able to nail down.

Heather stops me in the hall outside of her bedroom. "I've got to talk to you."

I narrow my eyes at her. "We already talked about this. There's nothing more to elaborate on."

Taking no for an answer should be something she accepts.

Heather opens up the bedroom door. "Come on and let's talk. I'll be sure to make it quick."

Brooke's got her hand around the necklace around her neck. It's a silver necklace with a diamond ring attached. Matt gave the ring and necklace to her the last time she saw him. "We're leaving before it gets cold out."

I shut the door behind me so the three of us can talk things through. "When did the two of you make this decision?"

Heather sits down on the bed and shakes her head. "There's no reason for the two of us to stay. If you're not going to give the two of us a chance, we've got to go out and find Matt."

My pulse quickens, but I'm not going to beg them to stay. Brooke does deserve to search for Matt. After all, he's the love of her life. If leaving will give her happiness, then it's what they should do. "I'll help you get a car out of town. Just tell me when you're going to leave."

Brooke grins. "I had a feeling you would agree to this."

I'm eager to see what Landon is up to. "Yeah, well, I got you out of the apartment. It was one of the worst places for the two of you to be. I'll let you have some guns and ammo.

Just don't go rushing out the door before saying goodbye first."

Heather wraps her arms around me, and I take a step back. Being touched by her isn't something I want. She could very well have something else up her sleeve.

I open up the bedroom door and then turn around. "Me or Landon will be back to put some boards over the windows."

Landon's in the bathroom putting up a board when I walk in. "These boards will make sleeping easier tonight."

"I was thinking the two of us could go out on the back porch tonight. You would be able to get a good night's rest, and I could make sure nobody comes in," I say.

To me it's the only thing to keep me sane tonight. I can't not take watch, even if the windows are boarded up. Somebody might not wake up in time if we were attacked. It's not a risk I'm willing to take.

He rubs his hand across his pant leg. "When you put things that way, I'll be spending my night looking up at the stars."

Maybe leaving him inside after he goes to sleep is a better idea. Being outside would have him tossing and turning all night.

"I miss those nights when we used to lay outside and stare up at the stars," I say.

It was just me and him lying on the porch in the warm summer air. I was drunk and would pass out before I even got in the door. Regardless of me being drunk, it was still a good time.

He laughs. "That night when that bear came out of the woods scared me shitless."

I grin real big. "I'm just glad it didn't have cubs."

I've never seen him come back inside the house so fast. It was the funniest shit ever. Thank God I was sober when it happened.

This world may be different now, but we can still make

good memories here. Not everything in this life is lost. Good things are still going to happen. Hell, Ava coming here is already something good within itself.

A bloodcurdling scream comes from outside. I fly out the back door and catch sight of Ava down by the outhouse. She's on the ground, and a zombie reaches down, trying to grab ahold of her.

Where the hell's Sunny at? This wasn't supposed to happen like this.

I get my gun out of my pants and shoot the zombie in the head. It goes down, and tears stream down Ava's face. I put my arms around her, and she sinks into them. " I'm here now," I say.

Sobs escape from her lips. "I dropped my knife on the ground."

I'm going to give her one of my guns. This can't happen again. I won't always be here to protect her.

"It's been a long day. Let's get you back inside so you can lay down," I say, helping her off the ground.

Sunny's standing by the camper and nods at Ava. "I see Joey came to your rescue."

I glare at him and shake my head in disgust. She could have been bitten and turned into a zombie. He should have been looking after her. "What the fuck were you doing just now?"

Sunny shrugs. "I had to take a piss. Turned around for literally two seconds."

I want to punch his fucking lights out, but I stop myself. This isn't something worth fighting over. We will discuss this later tonight or tomorrow. It's a conversation we need to have. "I hope you're going to keep your word with staying out here and keeping watch," I snap.

Sunny isn't fazed with me being upset with him. "Of course I'm going to. Ava's fine, and you just need to take a chill pill."

I walk away from him before I do something I'll regret. Tears are still streaming down Ava's face when we walk up the porch steps. Landon is waiting for us in the living room. His lips turn down in a frown. "What's going on?" he asks.

Ava pulls me towards the stairs. "A zombie was out there, and I dropped my knife."

Landon runs his hands through his hair. "Shit. At least you're okay now."

"Ava's fine, and it's what matters," I say.

Landon parts his lips. "I'm going to get back to boarding everything up."

"If you need me, you know where I'll be," I say.

When me and Ava get to my bedroom, she wipes the tears away with her hand. "I shouldn't be crying. Everything has just hit me all at once."

I lean back against the bed and close my eyes. Exhaustion sinks in, and a nap would do me some good. I'm not used to staying up all night anymore. I've got to have a couple of minutes of rest at least. "You have every reason to cry. You've been through a lot."

She presses her head against my chest. "I want to live a long time and have a peaceful death. Not one like Isabella and Angel."

I open up my eyes to stare into hers. "You're going to have to start firing a gun. It's a simple, quick, and easy way of taking down a zombie."

"What's going to happen when we run out of bullets?"

There will come a point in time when that happens. I just don't want to think about it right now.

I DIDN'T MEAN to get Joey all worked up earlier. Hell unlike Heather and Brooke, I like Ava. I wouldn't want anything to happen to her. It's not like I had my back away from her more than a couple of seconds. Didn't necessarily want her to see my dick. I've got to have some privacy.

The door opens to the house and Joey comes out. He stalks down to where I'm sitting, on top of the camper. "What the hell where you thinking earlier?"

Oh boy. Here we go.

I roll my eyes. "Can you just cut it out with this shit. I get it that you like her. I'm not going to steal her away from you."

I'll never be the type of man who steals his friend's girlfriend. I'm not that type of person and won't ever be.

He runs his hands through his hair. "It's just that I'm stressed out right now, since those people came here."

I get a cigarette out of my pocket and light it. "We can't worry about those people right now. Everyone's asleep and we'll both be out here taking watch."

He shakes his head. "I'm still concerned with what they're going to do next. I can't stay here tomorrow we've got to have food."

I take that first puff and the tension in my neck relaxes.

"Everything's out of your control. You shouldn't worry yourself sick over things."

He doesn't speak for several seconds and there's silence between us. "I hate that things have already come to this."

I flick the ashes on the ground below me. "You're doing the best you can. Heather, Brooke, Landon, and Ava are alive. That's saying something."

He slips a hand in his pocket. "You are right, they are alive and breathing. Things could be a lot worse."

Now we're finally getting somewhere. Now the Joey who's my friend is starting to come back around. I thought I had lost him there for a minute.

"I'll take care of those people tomorrow when you get back from that supply run," I say.

There's no reason for him to worry when I'll just take care of the problem.

He shakes his head. "I don't want you to do that."

I take another puff off my cigarette. "I don't give a fuck what you want. I'm doing it so your ass can stop worrying."

"I'm sorry about getting so upset with you."

I finish off my cigarette and then throw it down on the ground. "You've got nothing to be sorry about."

"I'm going to head out to the other side of the porch. I just wanted to tell you what was on my mind."

"Good night. You've got a good thing going with Ava so don't fuck it up."

I watch him leave and wish he would've stayed a little while longer. I'm not particularly fond of being all alone. It's when I begin to think about my little boy. The worst kind of pain is being inside my own head.

Regardless of Joey leaving I'm thrilled he didn't argue with me over going to look for those people. He probably realized it wasn't an argument he was going to win.

I don't know what tomorrow's going to bring with those people. The only thing I do know is I would've stayed back if it wasn't for Timmy. I wouldn't have run away like a scaredy cat. At the end of the day I'm not afraid to die. Guess that's why it doesn't bother me so much going back up there.

The leaves rustle and I get my gun out in front of me. My stomach tightens as I search around me looking for the source.

Make yourself be known. I'm ready to take you down.

My gaze lands on a deer behind me. I lower my gun prepared to kill the damn thing. This will be good to eat for breakfast. I put my finger on the trigger ready to fire. A baby fawn comes running behind the deer.

There's no way I'm killing the damn thing now. You can forget that shit.

Tears well up in my eyes and I push them back. Now isn't the time to cry. I'm a tough bastard who needs to stay strong. Even though staying strong is hard when you've lost almost everything you cared about.

The only good thing left in this world is Joey, Ava, and Landon. Heather and Brooke are okay but will never be my favorite people. I just hope I'll be able to take down those people tomorrow. So we can live at peace here on the farm like we deserve.

I WAKE up and touch the bed beside me. The sheets are empty and there's no way I'll be able to sleep without him beside me. It gives me comfort knowing he's so close by. I've got to go outside and keep watch beside him.

I light the candle and then get out of bed. My footsteps cause the hardwood floor to creak as I walk across it. The light from the candle acts as my guide as I stroll down the steps. It's so quiet in the house and chills run up my spine. Anything could have happened and me not known about it.

Stop it. Joey said he was going to keep you safe. He meant what he said.

I reach the back door and unlock it. A wave of relief washes over me when Joey turns around to glance at me. I step outside onto the porch and sit down beside him. "So how are things going? Have you seen anything out of the ordinary?" I ask.

He chuckles. "Everything's been alright. It actually just got a lot better since you're here."

I blow out the candle and give him a small smile. "Despite us being at odds with other people I'll never regret coming here. I would have never met you. You've welcomed me with open arms and made me feel at home."

He comes closer to me and wraps an arm around my shoulder. "I could've never turned you away. The look on your eyes the night you came did it for me. Your heart was broken and I wanted so desperately to make things better."

I cradle his face in my hands. "You have made everything better just by giving me a fighting chance. I'm sure other people would have turned me away in a heartbeat."

He stares into my eyes. "I'm just glad you came here and are with us. Other people might not be able to keep you safe. Not in the way I can because you're precious to me. You have my insides going out of control."

I close in the distance between the two of us and kiss his lips. A groan escapes from inside him and his hands go underneath my shirt. My breathing becomes heavy when he squeezes one of my breasts. I'm so wet I can hardly stand it. I've got to have more of him.

He sucks on my neck and it feels so good to be wanted. I reach for the buttons on his jeans and undo them. I need to feel every single part of him. Today has been hell and there's no promise of tomorrow.

The door opens and a familiar voice calls out. "Old man, well shit, I'm sorry I interrupted the two of you," Landon says.

I straighten myself up and unwind myself from Joey. "You didn't interrupt anything. I was just going upstairs and leaving."

Joey buttons up his jeans. "Ava, you're not going anywhere. The three of us need to talk."

Landon pulls at the collar of his shirt and sits down beside Joey. "I didn't really mean to interrupt anything."

I clear my throat. "I'm not going to beat around the bush. I like your father and the two of us are probably going to become a thing. It would be a mistake not to give the two of us a chance."

Joey grins. "It's good to know the two of us are on the same page."

Landon bites down on his bottom lip. "If I would've known the two of you were going to fuck I wouldn't have come out here. I can sure as hell take a hint but the two of you didn't say anything."

My face grows hot at his bluntness. "I'm glad you came out here. I can't ever be too careful, since I'm afraid of being pregnant. Being a mother isn't in the cards for me."

Joey rubs my back and I lean against him. "You saved the day by coming here if anything."

Landon shakes his head. "What time are we going on a run tomorrow?"

I'm glad he changed the subject so we don't have to talk about it anymore. It's a little strange and makes things awkward. Even though Landon now knows how the two of us feel about one another.

Joey lets out an exhausted sigh. "We'll leave tomorrow morning so we can go there and get back."

I hate thinking about the two of them being out there. I'll be worried all day thinking about them but there's nothing I can do about it. We've got to have food and supplies.

Landon leans back against the house and closes his eyes. "Where do you think we'll go?"

Joey interlaces his fingers with mine. My insides go wild at his touch. "I don't know, we'll find somewhere safe. Hope-fully we'll just have to go to the next county over."

Landon snores beside Joey. He must have really been tired.

"I hope the two of you won't be gone all day tomorrow," I say.

I'll be on the edge with them being gone. Not only that I'm not going to be crazy about being here with Heather and Brooke. Those crazy people are also still around.

Joey rubs my fingers and my insides are on fire. "We

shouldn't be but I would like for you to come with us. There's no reason for you to stay at the house with Heather and Brooke. The last thing I want is for things to be awkward for you."

I kiss his cheek and am now bubbling with happiness. "Thank you for letting me come along."

"After that kiss just now I don't want you to be out of my sight."

CHAPTER 29
JOEY

LANDON STRETCHES out his arms and legs. "I still can't believe I walked in on you guys last night."

Last night was beyond amazing it was fucking incredible. It's nice knowing Ava wants me as much as I want her. Not that I ever doubted that for a minute.

I'm a little bit embarrassed about what he did walk in on. Not that it was something that could be helped. "Don't worry about it. I didn't know it was going to happen."

He gets up and goes towards the door. "I'm going to see if Sunny's got breakfast started."

Good. I don't want to have this conversation any more than you do.

Ava stirs beside me and opens up her eyes. A smile crosses her lips when she sees me. "Last night was amazing if I must say so myself."

I give her a quick kiss on the lips. "It was every bit as amazing as I expected it to be. We're going to have to be more careful."

She laughs. "I didn't mean to attack you like that. It's just that I realize we don't know how much time we've got left together."

I hate hearing those words come out of her mouth even

though she's right. This world's uncertain and it's what hurts the most. "You're right we don't and am glad you did. My son didn't even really see anything bad. He won't be scarred for life."

Her belly begins to rumble. "I always stay so hungry."

I stand up and then grab ahold of her hand. "Let's go see what Sunny has ready for us to eat."

She pulls herself up and I lead the way through the house. Heather is in the hallway as we pass by and she flips me off. It doesn't make me angry or upset, because I have no shame in this. I'll never have any shame in going after what I want. I refuse to live my life with any regrets.

When we get back outside, Sunny is down at the bottom of the hill cooking. I'm not sure what he's got in his pot but it's bound to be something good. I'll eat almost anything these days since food is so scarce and hard to come by. I'm thankful for everything I've got.

Sunny's gaze goes towards Ava. "I didn't mean anything by not taking down that zombie last night."

Ava takes the bowl out of his hands. "Don't be silly. I'm alright and shouldn't have been stupid to begin with."

I'll get her one of my guns after we get finished eating. Then we'll head on out while it's still early. I'm not sure where we're going. My fingers are crossed nowhere too far. My sights are set on a grocery store in the next town over. Maybe we'll get lucky and it will be untouched.

Sunny shakes his head. "You're not stupid. Sometimes shit just happens."

I grab myself a bowl of the soup and spoon. "Come on. Let's go sit down in the garage and talk about a few things."

Landon's already in the garage stuffing his face full. "I'm going to get another bowl."

I want him to eat until he gets full. There's no telling when we'll get back.

Ava takes a bite of soup. "How long where you in the army for?"

Now's a good time to get to know one another. "Twenty years and it was more than enough for me. We moved around all the time and I felt guilty for always making Landon leave. He'd get so accustomed with making friends and then the army would make me go somewhere else."

Ava stops eating to narrow her eyes at me. "I'm sure he later understood the sacrifices that you made for him and everyone else."

I nod. "It still feels like I robbed him from friendships when he was a little boy. Brooke too when she came in the picture. I couldn't get out of the army since it's the only thing I've ever known."

She shakes her head. "You don't have a reason to feel guilty about anything. I'm sure looking back on everything now, Landon's so proud of you."

I let her words sink in. "Things weren't always that simple. I've grown accustomed to the words I hate you over the years."

She eats the rest of her food. "He was just a kid and didn't know what he was saying."

I blow on my food before taking a bite. "Those words made me regret ever having a career in the army. It made me wish I would've done something easier, so I could've been around more."

She rests her hand on my leg. I want nothing more than to bend her over and finish what we started last night. "You shouldn't feel that way. It's apparent how proud he is to be your son."

My chest is lighter since I told her what's been on my mind for a long time. It sure feels good to be able to talk her about anything.

I gulp down the rest of my food. "Come on. Let me go get you your gun."

She gives me a small smile and the two of us get up from the table. "I can't say I'm crazy about firing one."

"It's going to come in handy so don't ever be afraid to use it."

The two of us saunter up to the house and step inside. Heather and Brooke are nowhere to be seen. If I had a guess they're probably in their bedroom.

When the two of us get upstairs I get Ava a hand gun out of my bag. "Now you've got to move the hammer's switch to turn the safety on and off. You see that red dot there."

She stares intently at the gun. "Does that mean it's ready to fire?"

For someone who doesn't like guns she knows quite a bit.

I move the switch to the other side, so that the gun's safety is on. "It does so make sure you always keep the safety on unless you intend to use it."

She takes the gun from me and puts it in her pants. "I've got to brush my teeth then I'll be ready to go."

"Promise me you won't ever be afraid to use that gun."

"You better believe I'll use it if it's life or death."

Her saying that gives me comfort.

IT SHOULD GIVE me comfort having a loaded gun in my pants. I just wish things didn't come to this. The world is so evil. I've got to get used to it and the way people are.

Joey brushes his teeth quickly beside me. "I'll be outside when you're ready to come down."

I put toothpaste on my toothbrush. "I'll be down in just a couple of minutes."

He kisses my forehead before going out the door.

I brush my teeth enjoying every minute of how refreshed my mouth is. It might seem crazy but taking care of my teeth is something that will always matter to me. Nothing about that will ever change.

I spit in the sink and then wipe it out with a washcloth. Now I'm ready to go and do this. It's going to be nice being with Joey and Landon. Better than staying here with Brooke and Heather any day. Now that I've kissed Joey, I expect things to be more awkward than ever between all of us. It sucks things have come to that.

I walk out of the bathroom and meet Brooke in the hallway. She glares back at me. "If this was my house, you'd never be welcome here," she snaps.

Don't say anything back to her. It's what she wants. Just walk down the steps like nothing's happened.

I grin. "I hope you have a good day today."

Brooke presses her lips together, and a scowl appears on her face. She lets out a sigh of frustration.

I put my hand on the railing and roll my eyes. It's hard keeping my composure with her even though it's the right thing to do. Her hands shove my back, and I steady myself on my feet. If my hand wasn't on the rail, I would've fallen and possibly gotten hurt.

Brooke goes past me with a smirk on her face. "By the time it's all over, you're going to wish you'd never come."

Chills run up and down my spine at the threat. This is something I'm going to tell Joey about. She is dead set on harming me. There's no telling what else she'll do.

I reach the bottom of the steps and then run out the door. Joey is down by the fire pit talking to Sunny. My heart races out of my chest as I go to join the two of them. "Can we talk?" There's urgency in my voice.

Joey grabs ahold of my hand, and we start walking towards the road. "What's going on?"

I look down at the ground and then meet his eyes. "It's Brooke. I'm afraid of her."

His green eyes widen. "I'm not sure what you mean by that."

I let the words slip out of my mouth. "She tried to push me down the stairs and threatened me."

He paces on the road and shakes his head in disgust. "It's a damn good thing you're going with us."

Maybe it's best if you don't let things escalate with Joey.

I saunter back towards Sunny and don't say anything else to him. Joey grabs ahold of my arm, and I stop walking. "Maybe this between the two of us isn't meant to be."

He sways forward and raises his eyebrows. "You're going to let the two of them get in the way of us. I'm not having it, and you shouldn't either. Don't let them win. This is what they want."

I let out a sigh of frustration and bite my lower lip. "I don't even know if I'm good in bed."

He laughs. "Last night you were fucking incredible. I'm sure you're perfectly fine."

My face grows hot, and I playfully punch his arm. "Another thing about last night. We didn't have any condoms. We've got to have some if we have sex."

He rubs my back, and my insides come alive. "Who said anything about needing condoms?"

My lips turn up into a smile. "I did. I can't ever get pregnant."

It's too risky in this world. I would be worried the entire nine months. If something were to go wrong, a nurse or doctor wouldn't be there to help me.

His face turns serious. "Okay. We'll make sure to always use protection."

I haven't used the bathroom all morning and I'm about to bust now. "I've got to relieve my bladder."

A toilet is something I'll always miss. I have to take a piss as soon as I wake up every morning. It's something I don't ever expect to change.

He puts his hand through mine. "I'll be your lookout."

I swing my arms as the two of us walk. There's nothing quite like being able to use the bathroom in peace. "So what's your favorite position?"

His eyes light up at the mention of us fucking. "I always like being on top."

Butterflies form in my stomach as I think about him naked going down on me. "That's good to know, for when the time comes."

Music blasts through the air, a sure indicator of someone coming. Pee trickles into my panties, and I open the outhouse door. I shut it behind me and relieve my bladder. Thankfully, the urine was only a couple of drops.

My heart races when I crack the door open.

Joey has his gun out in front of him. "Stay back. I've got this handled."

A man with red hair and a goatee steps out of the driver's side. "Joey, I'll be damned. You're just the man I want to see."

I PUT MY GUN AWAY, and a grin creeps on my face. "It's good seeing you, Wyatt. Didn't know if you were still alive."

Me and Wyatt were in the army together. We went through basic training and have been friends ever since. Every year we try to hang out and catch up. Even though sometimes we can't since he lived in California. Which makes me wonder why he's in these parts now.

Wyatt snorts. "This apocalypse isn't putting me in the ground. You should know better than that."

I'm not bullshitting around with him. Now isn't the time for us to have a long conversation. There's a reason he's here, and I want to know why.

"It's nice to see you, but what the hell do you want?" I couldn't be more blunt if I wanted to.

Wyatt spits the chewing tobacco out of his mouth. "I want you to help me with something."

This could be a good thing. He could know a place to get supplies.

The base of my neck tingles, and I edge my way closer to him. "You can go ahead and elaborate on that."

A smirk forms on Wyatt's face. "My woman was kidnapped and I'm trying to get her back."

Fuck. This isn't a fight we need to get involved in. But then again, he's one of your oldest friends. He'd do anything for you. It's only right to return the favor.

Landon steps out of the garage, probably to see what's going on. "Shit, man. It's been too long since I've seen you."

Wyatt chuckles. "It's good to see you, Landon."

I turn to Ava, who's silent beside me. "This is Wyatt one of my oldest friends and we're going with him into the town."

She licks her lips. "Okay. I'm ready."

Me and Ava jog over to where Wyatt's standing. "Let's go. We can talk on the road."

Landon makes himself comfortable in the front seat. "I'm glad we're leaving the farm for a while. Those people have me scared shitless."

I put an arm around Ava. "We've been having trouble with the house on the top of the hill."

Wyatt pulls out of the driveway, and we start our journey towards town. "It's no surprise to me about the group. I've been out there in South Carolina and North Carolina. Let's just say you're lucky you've got this farm."

We are lucky, and it's the reason I don't ever want to leave.

I clear my throat. "How did you end up so close by?"

Wyatt stares out at the road with an unreadable expression on his face. "We moved to South Carolina before the apocalypse happened. Tammi wanted to be closer to her mother and father."

The time we were in the military, Tammi always loved spending time with her family. Especially since her and Wyatt never did have any children.

"I'm glad you came searching for me. It's nice having so many familiar faces around," I say.

Wyatt's lips turn down in a frown. "I came looking for you since you're the only person I've got left. Tammi was killed when we lived in South Carolina."

My body is on fire, and the only thing I can see is a flash of red. Tammi never deserved to die like that. There's no doubt in my mind Wyatt handled the situation. It's absolutely sickening how evil people can be.

Ava shifts in her seat and stares out the window. A frown's on her face and I can't help but wonder what she's thinking about.

I reach out and squeeze his shoulder. "You'll always have a place at the farm."

Wyatt grips the steering wheel. "It took everything inside me not to pull the trigger on myself. Marla, a woman I met in South Carolina, saved my life. She took me under her wing and stopped me."

Everything's starting to click clearly now. Marla must be the woman being held hostage. I'll do whatever I can to help him with getting her back. He's one of my oldest friends and wouldn't lie to me.

I've got to find out more about the story. So I know what we're up against. "What exactly happened with her?" I ask.

Wyatt takes a right turn towards town. "We were searching for food, and some guys didn't want us in the grocery store. I shot one of them dead so we could get what we needed. More of them showed up, and it's when I knew I'd made a mistake."

Great. This is more than what I was expecting. It makes perfect sense since we weren't able to go into the grocery store. These people who think they can control everything have another thing coming to them.

"Are we still going to be able to get food today?" Landon asks.

"Of course we are. I didn't come out all this way not to get what we need," I answer.

The same woman is still strolling around down there at the track. Today she's got on a pair of sandals and a dress. This is more than likely the place she's staying. There's a small bathroom on the facility with the playground. That's not even mentioning the pool, which has a concession stand and bathrooms. It would just be freezing at wintertime.

A car pulls out in front of us and makes its way down to the walking track. A car load of men get out of the vehicle. An inferno burns inside me at what they're going to do to her. Wyatt keeps driving and it makes me feel like a terrible person. We should've taken those men down. The thing about it is we don't know that woman.

"We've got plenty of food and supplies, I'm willing to share," Wyatt chimes in.

Tears stream down Ava's face and I hold her close to me. "I wish we could have stopped to save her," she says.

I press my lips against her forehead. "We can't save everyone, that's the tough part about being a human being."

Wyatt rolls his eyes. "What's your name? I've never seen you around before."

She sobs uncontrollably against me. "I'm Ava and you must not be anything like Joey," she chokes out.

Landon's lips are turned down in a frown. "Right when I thought today was going to be a good day."

"It is going to be a good fucking day. I've got supplies and food I'm willing to share," Wyatt says.

The tension in my neck relaxes as a weight has been lifted off my shoulders. We're not going to have any problem with making it back by nightfall.

"You showed up just in time because we were running low on everything," I reply.

Wyatt pulls into the parking lot of the old pharmacy. "Let's load up the car so we can head back to the farm and get Marla."

I'm more than ready to do this. We can't get back to the farm soon enough. "Did I mention how happy I am that you came to find us?" I ask.

I CAN'T BELIEVE Joey's agreed to let other people come here. Doesn't make any damn sense. Even though Wyatt may be his friend. It's just stupid letting people we don't know come in here and be around all of us. It will never settle well with me.

Brooke and Heather are in their bedroom. Have been in there ever since everyone left. I don't have a clue of what they're doing. As long as they keep their distance from me, I'm perfectly happy.

There's no use me trying to sleep with everyone being gone. I'm too on the edge even though boards are over all the windows downstairs. It's not enough to give me comfort. If someone wants to get in they will regardless.

I refuse to be holed up in the house all damn day. The outdoors is where I like to be.

I go outside and sit down on the porch steps. Hopefully, Joey comes back soon. I'm not in the mood to be here with Heather or Brooke. Since I don't like them I'm obviously not going to converse with them. Which makes me feel all alone.

Nathan comes to my mind and I slap myself in the head. I can't think about him, not now.

Those people are still up here at that house. Right now I'm

all alone. Joey can't run his damn mouth and tell me not to go. I'm going back up there and going to prowl around. It's not going to hurt anything. I can take some of his ammo and guns. Blast them fucking people off the face of the earth. Then we won't have a problem with them anymore.

When Timmy was with me I had his life to think about. Well, before he went and fucked up his ankle. Now the only person's life I have to think about is myself. I'm not sitting here going stir crazy when shit needs to be done.

I march back into the house and knock on Heather's door. She opens it just enough for me to see her face. "I'm leaving so you need to lock the doors," I declare.

Her mouth falls open and she gapes at me. "You're really going to leave me and Brooke here by ourselves?"

Yeah you fucking bitch you're a grown woman.

"I'll grab you one of Joey's guns from upstairs," I say.

Her lip trembles and she frowns. "I'm coming with you."

I don't say anything as the two of us make our way up the stairs.

She bends down in the closet and grabs one of the guns. "I can't believe you're doing this to us."

Save it bitch. You know I've never liked you after what you did to Joey.

I grab some bullets for my gun and put them in my pocket. "I've got to find out what I can about those people. I'm not going to sit here twiddling my fingers."

"I hope you're able to take care of the problem then," she says before going out the bedroom door.

You're wrong I do.

Adrenaline runs through my body as I saunter down the hall to get a rifle out of the gun cabinet. Now it's time to go.

I knock on the bedroom door. "I'm going and it would be best if you locked the door behind me."

"Don't worry I will," Heather replies back through the door.

I hurry outside and get in my truck. There's no way in hell I'm walking through the woods. I'll take my truck out to the end of the road and then walk up to the house. I've got nothing to lose. All of my family is dead.

I put the key in the ignition and pull out of the driveway. My heart stammers at what's coming next. One thing that's for certain is me not fearing death. I'm not sure where I'll go when I die. Hopefully it's some place that my little boy and wife will be.

I park my truck beside the car at the end of the driveway. Then turn off the engine. I grab the rifle and start my journey up to my house. My shoes crunch against the gravel driveway and an engine roars to life nearby.

A tightness forms in my stomach and I run behind a big tree out of harm's way.

The van comes by me several seconds later. I'm unable to tell how many people are in it.

I step out from behind the tree and continue making my way up the hill. There's not a single soul outside and no other vehicles are around. Now's the time to score the area and see what I can find.

My gaze lands on the barn that's situated a couple of yards from me. It'll be a good place to check out.

Go in there nice and slow.

I put my gun in front of me and open up the barn door. My eyes widen since there's a woman in front of me. Her hands are tied and she's got tape over her mouth. "What the fuck," I say.

Anger erupts inside of me at what they're going to do to her. I've got to get her out of here before they come back.

I prop the rifle up on the ground beside her and get a pocket knife out of my pocket. "Don't you worry about those people now I'm getting you out of here."

Tears stream down her face but she's unable to say anything because of the tape over her mouth.

"This must hurt a little," I say before pulling the tape off of her mouth.

Terror is in her brown eyes. "We've got to get out of here. This guy who's taking watch is still here. The rest of them went out town looking for more victims."

I cut through the rope and untie her hands. "Who are these fucking people anyway?"

She shakes her head. "I've stuck to myself. They kidnapped me from the walking track."

"Let's go. I've got a truck at the bottom of the hill," I say.

I'm glad I came up here. By doing so I probably saved her life.

She gets up from the ground and beads of sweat drip down her forehead. "We've got to be careful," she says over and over again.

It's apparent in her words that she doesn't want to die. I just hope she trusts me to keep her safe.

I pick up the rifle and point it in front of me. "Stay behind me."

She does what I say and her breathing's heavy. "They were planning on killing me tonight."

There's tension in the back of my neck. It's pathetic those fuckers killing people for fun.

I cautiously stroll out of the barn and glance around me. The only thing I can see is the house some yards away and the road. Nobody else is around unless they are hiding. "Stay close behind me."

Her hands grip onto my shirt.

I let out a sigh in frustration.

I didn't mean to actually grab ahold of me.

A bullet shoots past me and I look around searching for the source. "Let the woman go. She belongs to all of us now."

The inferno inside of me is about to be unleashed. "The woman doesn't belong to anyone. She's not going to become your victim. So you better show yourself instead of hiding like some fucking coward."

She gets down on her knees to save herself. "He's up there in one of the trees by the house," she whispers.

Another round sails through the air and it narrowly misses my leg. I divert my gaze in the direction where it's coming from. My eyes land on him and I shut my eye before locking in on his head. A couple of seconds pass by, before I can get a clear shot.

Stay right there mother fucker.

I press my finger on the trigger and pull the trigger. The bullet smacks into his head and he goes down. A wave of happiness washes over me because this fucker's dead. "We've got to make it down to the road."

She stands up and her eyes blink rapidly. "The others will be back soon. We need to hurry."

I stroll down the road as fast as I can. "Was he all alone?"

She nods. "He's the only one who stays back when they go out."

At least right now we don't have to worry about those other people.

The two of us walk in silence for a couple of minutes. My mind's going a lot of different directions. I killed one of theirs. It's a fact they're going to be making their way to us today. "I'm Sunny. What's your name?"

The two of us round a bend and soon we'll be to the truck.

She clears her throat. "Kallie and I can't believe you saved me."

I shrug. "I came up there looking for all of them and found you."

The truck's up ahead and a wave of relief washes over me. We made it back safe and sound.

She saunters over to the truck ahead of me and freezes. "We're not going to be going anywhere."

I wrinkle my nose and approach her. "Why the hell is that?"

She narrows her eyes at me. "The tires are slit."

The worst part about it is, I don't know, if the people that drove off in the van did this, or someone else.

I'M NOT crazy about being here with Wyatt. It hurts my soul he didn't stop for that poor woman. I can only think the worst has happened to her.

I get out of the car eager to fill it with supplies. It will be nice to not leave the farm for awhile. Now we just need to take care of those people on the hill then we'll be doing alright.

Joey has already made his way inside. He's insisted on going in there with Wyatt first.

Landon's hands are in his pockets. "I'm glad you're with my dad. He seems at ease with you around."

I give him a small smile. "I'm glad I am too. Even though we barely know each other."

Joey comes out of the pharmacy with his jaw in a tight line. "Everything's gone. We've got nothing left to take with us."

My heart sinks that someone raided out this place. It's a damn shame now we've got to go searching for food. "Where are we going now?" I ask.

Wyatt storms out of the pharmacy. "We're heading to the grocery store. My group was supposed to be here. I'm going to blow all those fuckers off the face of the earth."

I don't think that sounds like such a great idea. Even though my opinion doesn't matter. Wyatt's going to do whatever he wants regardless of what I have to say. "You're putting all of our lives at stake here for your own benefit."

Joey takes a step back. "What the fuck are you talking about other people? You never mentioned having a group before."

Wyatt rolls his eyes. "Get in the fucking car unless you want to be stranded here in the parking lot."

I get in the car the anger rushing through me all at once. This Wyatt guy isn't who he has said to be. It's absolutely ridiculous being here for no good reason. Now we've got to another place that could potentially be dangerous. Not my idea of a good day.

Joey's veins pop out of his neck as he slams the door shut behind him. "Don't know what the fuck I was thinking trusting him. I wonder what else he's hiding from us."

Landon's lips are turned down in a frown when he gets in the car. "Old man you and I both know he's completely harmless."

My mind goes to what Wyatt said about his wife. "Maybe this world has changed him."

Wyatt gets in the car and puts an end to our conversation. "I didn't think you'd let all of us stay at the farm."

I'm sure Joey would have let all of his people live at the farm. It's no excuse for him to keep that from him.

Joey laughs without humor. "So you're just now springing that on me. You should have mentioned it from the get go."

There's zombies walking along the sidewalk and it makes me shudder. I can't imagine being stuck out here with all of them. The farm is my safety net and I'm so grateful to call it my home.

"I didn't know what you were going to fucking say," Wyatt barks.

This conversation is getting us nowhere so I drown it out.

My main concern is us getting food and supplies. We better get some before we head back to the farm. I'll definitely be speaking my mind about it if we don't.

Joey shakes my arm. "Ava, we're here at the grocery store."

I stare at the grocery store and it looks completely empty. There's no one on top of the roof or standing outside. Only a few members of the undead roam around in the parking lot. I don't think anyone is here. So maybe it's a good thing.

Wyatt gets out of the car and slams the door shut. "This is the worst day of my fucking life! I planned on killing me some fucking bastards and they're not here!"

I don't know what good screaming is going to do. It's only going to direct attention to all of us. "Should we bother going inside?" I turn to Joey who's standing beside me.

Joey shakes his head. "When we were here a couple of days ago, this place was surrounded. He's just got to get ahold of himself before we leave."

I'm not sure how long that's going to take. Hopefully Joey can help him be in his right mind. "I hope you've not forgotten about us needing supplies."

"I haven't forgotten anything," he whispers.

Landon hasn't stepped foot outside the car. It seems like a good idea to join him.

A woman peeks her head out from behind the bank. She points her gun at me. "It looks like it's my lucky day don't move."

There's no way in hell I'm shooting her. I don't know who she is or anything she wants. Hell Joey or Wyatt will end her life so I won't have to. "None of us are here to harm you," I began to say.

Joey's two steps ahead of me. "Let her go or things aren't going to end well for you."

The woman doesn't budge with putting down her gun.

"I've been through hell these past couple of days. That ends today. I'm not afraid to take your life."

Wyatt's mouth drops open. "Marla, you're alive? I didn't think I would ever see you again."

Marla lowers her gun and a grin forms on her face. "They started loading everything and some kid helped me escape. I've never seen so many people there my entire life."

Wyatt wraps his arms around her in a hug. "Where did everyone go?"

Marla's face falls and her lips tremble. "The farm."

My mind goes to Sunny, Brooke, and Heather. We've got to get back and save them. A lump forms in my throat. We may already be too late.

CHAPTER 34

SUNNY

I ROLL my neck and have my gun trained in front of me when we start walking down the road. My thoughts go to Heather and Brooke who are still in the house. If someone came to the door I hope they sure as hell fired that gun. Maybe none of those people are around. Sure as hell hope they're not.

Kallie rubs her hands across her shorts. "I take it you live down here."

I nod. "It's my friend Joey's house but yeah we do."

Kallie stares out at the road in front of us. "I was staying down there in the pool concession stand. It was awful lonely being there by myself."

I just saved her fucking life. It's not going to hurt anything to learn more about her. "How long have you been down there?"

Sadness washes over her face. "A couple of weeks. My boyfriend got bit by a zombie the day we decided to stay. I didn't leave because I've got no car or anything at all."

It seems like we're all fucked up or have endured shit. I'm starting to believe that's the shitty part of life now. I lower the gun since I don't see anything. "I'm sorry about your boyfriend," I say.

She raises her eyebrows and stares at me. "Have you got any family around?"

I'm not going to talk about my little boy or wife with her. I don't want to be sad or angry right now. It will be nice to just not feel anything. "All the people who live here are my family now," I say.

It's not like I'm telling some lie. I've known Joey for what seems like forever. We're close and I consider him the brother I never had.

She nods. "I'm glad you've got people you care about and love still around."

I don't know what to say to that so I keep my mouth shut.

We go around a corner and I can see the house out of the corner of my eye. "We're here if you want to take a look around."

Her eyes light up and she strolls quickly up the porch's steps. "This house is beautiful. I hope there's room for me. At least for a little while until I get back on my feet."

I knock on the door. Hopefully, Heather hears me and will let us in. "That would be up to Joey and not me."

Hell Joey let Ava stay here. He's also letting that other group stay here. Don't see why he wouldn't let Kallie.

She has an uncomfortable look on her face. "I thought your family was here. Why are you knocking on the door?"

Heather's got to be in there. I don't know why she won't get up to answer it.

I press my lips together and narrow my gaze at her. "They are here. Please don't start asking me a bunch of questions. I'm not in the mood for it."

She rubs her face with her hand. "I won't ask you anything."

Several seconds pass by of silence between us.

Heather comes to the door and unlocks it. "I could hardly hear you out here."

That's not anything but a fucking lie.

I step inside of the house. "This is Kallie and I found her up there by the house."

Heather stares down at the floor and I sense something is wrong. "Joey's probably going to be gone awhile. She should just make herself at home."

I hate to admit it but Heather's right. "Kallie, go ahead and have a seat at the kitchen table."

Kallie puts her hands over her mouth. "I can't go in there. He's going to kill me."

A gun clicks from behind me. "Don't try anything. You're outnumbered there's more of us here than of you," a male's voice echoes through my ears.

I turn around and stare at the fucker. He's got gray hair and ice-cold green eyes. There's nothing more that I want to do than smash his skull in. I'm tempted to since he could be bluffing for all I know. "Leave these women alone. They didn't do anything to you. I'm the one who killed your friend. I enjoyed every minute of watching him bleed out."

The guy stares at me with his devilish smirk. "You try anything everyone here is dead. I suggest you put the gun down."

Don't do it. He's bluffing. You can take him down in a heartbeat.

I challenge him with my eyes. "I'm not fucking afraid of you."

The guy throws back his head and laughs. "You should be afraid of me."

A scream echoes through the house and I look around searching for the cause. The fiery rage consumes me and my demons are about to take over. "What is your fucking problem?" I lower my gun at him, more than ready to blast him off of the face of the earth.

Heather bites down on her bottom lip. "Please do what he says. They've got Brooke."

Kallie runs out the door to save herself and the asshole

goes running after her. Deep down I know things aren't going to end well for her. She's got nowhere else to go.

I want to shoot him but I hold back. If they've got Brooke like Heather says, I could be putting her life in jeopardy. "How many of them are here?" I say so only she can hear.

Heather's not able to respond because a woman saunters down the steps. Two men appear in the kitchen and one of them has a gun pressed against Brooke's forehead. Her lips quiver and she flares her nostrils.

The man who has his grip on Brooke tightens his hold. "Put the gun down before her brains are splattered all over the floor."

There could be more of them here than what's present. As bad as I hate to I set the gun on the floor. These fuckers must have been watching us. It's the only thing I can come up with. "I'm the one you should be after, "I snap.

The woman comes over to Heather and touches her hair. "We don't want just you. We've got to take all of you. This house is something that soon will be ours."

You're wrong you fucking bitch. This house will never belong to all of you.

"What's wrong with the house you've got up there?" I ask.

The woman smirks at me revealing her yellow-stained teeth. "It's not big enough."

A gunshot rings out in the hair and my heart sinks. I'm certain Kallie's dead. My rage ignites to the surface. It takes everything inside me to not lose control. "So what's your plan to kill us all then?" I snap.

I'll find a way for us to get out of this mess before that happens. Brooke and Heather aren't dying on my watch.

The man who hasn't spoken narrows his eyes at me. "The three of you are going to play a little game."

Yeah right. I'm not playing anything you sick freak.

Brooke thrashes around and screams. "Let go of me!"

The door swings open and the man who was outside with

Kallie comes in. He comes straight to me. "She's dead and I'm going to make sure you're next."

He killed her for no good reason. I lose control of myself and push him against the wall. "You no good piece of shit. She didn't do anything to you!"

A gun hits me on the back of the head and I completely black out.

CHAPTER 35
SUNNY

I OPEN up my eyes and there's a pounding in my head. Would be nice to have a cigarette. There's women and men who are unfamiliar to me. I don't know who the fuck they are or where I am. My hands are tied behind my back and it infuriates me to no end.

"Why the fuck are we all here?" I ask.

Maybe if I talk and ask questions someone will say something back.

A woman shakes beside me. "We're here because they're going to feed us to zombies."

Chills run up and down my spine. There's no way I'm dying at the hands of a zombie. I've got to find a way to get out of here. "Do you know where we are?" I ask.

The woman shakes her head. "I've never been this far back in the mountain."

Maybe we're in a house close by to Joey's. There's several more houses along the road other than his. Either way it's not something I'm worried about right now. My main concern is getting the fuck out of here.

I glance around the room to see if there's any way for me to get my hands free. There's only a wall and other than that the room's completely empty.

Fuck. Something's got to give.

If I talk then maybe I'll be able to figure out something I don't know. "Do you know who these people are?"

Her brown eyes go wide. "We've been at ends with them the past couple days. Wyatt killed one of theirs and things haven't been the same since. They came to the place we were staying and murdered two men right in front of us."

Sounds like they've had a horrible time. No wonder Wyatt came here earlier this morning. He's part of the reason why we're in this mess. "You listen to me. We're getting out of this alive."

She nods but looks down at the floor. It makes me think she doesn't believe me. "Those women that came here with you are outside."

I'm glad she let me know. When it comes to bail the two of them are going with me.

The door opens and the man who walks in was at the house earlier. I'd recognize him from anywhere since I want to beat the smugness off of his face. "You're coming with me," there's a hint of a smile in his voice.

He grabs ahold of my arm and drags me out the door. The house is in the distance and the barn's right in front of us. I must have come out of an old wine cellar or something.

I want more than anything to knock him out. If I knew more about all the people here I most definitely would. I grit my teeth as we keep moving forward. "You're making a big mistake by doing this," I bark.

He laughs like I've said something comical. "Sounds to me like you're trying to be a tough guy with those accusations."

I'd rather be a tough guy than a pathetic piece of shit.

I walk past Heather and Brooke who are both tied up against a tree. Their eyes look like they're going to bulge out of their head. "You've got to get us out of here," Heather mouths to me.

I act like I don't pay any attention to her as I pass by.

The man pushes me forward and presses a gun against my back. "Now you're going to stand here with me, and watch what's going to happen to you."

My body tenses up as I watch two men carry a woman out of the house. She's a petite woman not older than twenty-five. The man beside me begins to laugh. "We're just getting to the good part."

The men set her down and she glances around at all of us. "You're about to join your Maker. How do you feel about that?" The man with the ball cap on his head asks.

Tears stream down her face and the terror is in her eyes. "Please I've not done anything to you."

The guy with red hair glares at her. "You exist and that's more than enough."

The man with the ball cap pushes her and she falls to the ground. "Tell everybody to come outside. It's time to get started with this fun."

Keaton, the guy with red hair hurries off. It makes me wonder what those fuckers are going to do. I don't under-stand any of this because I'm not like them. I've killed before but being around them makes me realize I'm not some sort of psycho.

I stare up at the sky and Nathan appears. Angel wings are wrapped around his body. Tears are streaming down his face. "Daddy, you're going to survive this world. These people need you to help them."

A lump forms in my throat. "I should've been able to help you. We shouldn't have gone to the movies that night."

Nathan shakes his head. "Daddy, you've got to accept that it was my time to die."

I flare my nostrils and reach out. I've got to grab ahold of him. "No, you should still be alive."

Nathan waves at me. "I love you Daddy and you've got to be strong."

A tear streams down my face. "I'll always love you son."

Nathan disappears in the clouds out of sight.

The guy with the ball cap laughs in my face. "Damn and I thought I was crazy."

It takes everything in my power not to head butt him. "Something wouldn't be right if this world didn't make us all crazy."

The guy continues to laugh. "Maybe we should let you be one of our own."

I'd be dead in my grave before that happens.

I watch as people begin making our way to where we're standing. There's a couple of kids and one little boy who reminds me of Nathan. He almost looks like the spitting image of him. The only difference is this little boy has black hair.

There's about thirty people here and that's more than I care to think about. It's a hell of a lot more people than what I thought. With so many of them here it's going to be hard to escape.

You can do this Daddy. Your time on earth isn't over yet.

Keaton strolls towards the barn with a big grin on his face. "Folks it's time for us to watch these people be ripped apart. We can't live in this world with them. It's impossible after the hell we've encountered when it comes to them."

Cheers come out from the crowd and I shake my head in disgust. There will never be any peace until all these people are dead. The little boy who looks like my Nathan's lips are turned down in a frown. He must realize what they're doing isn't right.

Two guys go over to where the woman's sitting on the ground. "We're going to love them ripping you apart," one man says.

The woman thrashes her feet even though it's no use. They're far more powerful than she is. My heart aches at knowing what this poor woman's fate is. At least it's going to buy me some time, to devise a plan to escape.

The inferno surges through my chest but I can't focus on that. I've got to stay focused on staying alive. If I don't me, Heather, and Brooke are going to be next.

The guy who had the gun pressed up against my back moves closer towards the barn. I suspect the sick freak wants to see everything up close.

I glance around the area and no one seems to pay me any mind. Their eyes are locked towards that barn. They are spawns of Satan who take pleasure in seeing people hurt and in pain.

The little boy who looks like my Nathan comes over to where I'm standing. "Mister, listen to me loud and clear," his voice is so low I can barely hear him.

I kneel down to his level. "Can you help me get out of here? My friends and I are in trouble," I whisper.

"You're not going to be able to save them all. You need to save yourself," the boy tells me.

I've got no reason to save anyone but Heather and Brooke. I hate to leave these innocent lives here at the hands of these people. I don't have any choice.

I tilt my head to the side and raise my eyebrows. "You going to help me get out of here?"

The little boy nods. "I've got a knife in my pocket."

You remind me so much of my little boy. It's almost like you're his ghost.

The barn door opens and one by one the undead comes out of the barn. They must have gotten these fucking zombies after I had left earlier. The poor woman lets out a sheer shriek as the terror of what's about to happen rips through her body.

I turn away unable to watch the zombies rip the woman apart. "You ready to cut me loose, kid?"

The little boy cuts through the rope and my hands go free. "Me and my friends have got you covered. Get out of here while you can."

I press a palm to my chest. "I've got to cut those women loose by the tree."

The little boy hands me the knife. "Don't waste another second, you've not got much time."

I take a deep breath and glance all around me. Everyone's eyes are still glued to the woman who's being tortured. My heart batters against my chest as I casually stroll over to where Heather and Brooke are.

Tears stream down Heather's face. "Thank God you're here. I thought we were all done for."

We aren't out of the woods yet. We've still got to get the fuck out of here undetected.

I cut through the rope as a high-pitched scream rings out across the mountain. "We're going behind the house and into the woods," I say in a low voice.

Brooke's mouth falls open and her upper lip curls back. She's frozen in time at what's unfolding before her eyes.

Heather shakes Brooke and her eyes go wide. "We've got to go and I mean now," Heather's voice is urgent.

Brooke blinks rapidly. "We can't end up like her," she stammers on her words.

I casually stroll towards the back of the house. "Stay close to me."

A woman I don't recognize stares at the three of us suspiciously. "You're going the wrong way. Don't you want to have some excitement in your life?"

Watching innocent people be ripped to shreds isn't my idea of excitement.

"We've got to use the bathroom," I reply gripping onto the scissors that are in my hand.

Nice and easy don't let her realize who you are.

She takes a step back. "Go ahead then I'm not watching."

Brooke's body trembles and the fear's written in Heather's eyes.

Don't either of you take off running. It will blow our cover.

The three of us keep edging our way towards the woods. It's only a couple of feet away and within our grasp.

We've just got to take a few more steps.

A gun rings out through the air. "Three people have gone missing! Two women and a man with shaggy brown hair! We've got to find them and bring them back here! Their lives end today!"

We've got to run like we're escaping from the depths of hell.

I take off running through the woods with Heather and Brooke close behind me. A bullet flies past me and adrenaline shoots through my veins. We can't stop for anything until we're certain they're not following us.

Brooke slips over a tree branch and falls. "I can't believe this is happening right now. Please don't leave me Sunny. Me and Mom won't survive without you."

I glance back at the woman who shot the gun. The kid who saved our lives bites down on her leg. She screams out in agony and blood drips from his lips. He's buying us time so we can get out of this alive.

Get the fuck up Brooke. You can do this.

"Baby get up please. I can't live in this world without you," Heather pleads.

"I'll help you find Matt once this shit is over," I reply.

Brooke reaches for my hand and I help her up. "I'm sorry for acting the way I did," Brooke says.

Now's not the time to apologize. We've got to keep moving.

"Can you walk on that leg?" I ask hoping the answer is yes.

Brooke limps but walks just fine. "It hurts like hell but I can."

Another round sails past me and this time I don't look back. We've got to keep moving faster. We can't let them catch us or we'll be dead in our graves. That little boy and his friends can only stop so much.

A shiver runs down my spine as I think about what those people would do to us. We've got to pick up the pace and I mean now. "Come on. We're almost down by the river."

Brooke hobbles on her leg and winces in pain. "I'm going as fast as I can."

I listen closely to the rustling of leaves. A zombie comes out from behind a tree. The remains are of what used to be a man. The undead's teeth chatter and his arms are outstretched in front of him.

Startled screams escape from Heather's and Brooke's lips. The two of them take a step back and lean up against a tree.

The zombie takes a step towards me. I search the ground desperate to find anything to smash the brains in. My eyes land on a rock by the zombie's decaying foot. I crawl down on the ground to retrieve it.

Take this mother fucker.

I grab ahold of the rock as the rage rushes out of me at once. The rock slams down into the zombie's head hard and brains splatter on me. Now we've got to keep moving.

Heather and Brooke follow me through the thick over-grown brush.

My heart feels like it's going to explode and I struggle to catch a breath. Sweat drips down my forehead from the sun's warm rays. The sound of the waterfall lets me know we're close to the road.

Brooke bends over trying to catch her breath. "My leg's throbbing and I need a break."

We've got to keep going.

"We're almost there," I declare.

Heather rubs Brooke's shoulder. "Dig deep inside baby. We don't have time to rest."

Brooke nods. "I'm ready. Let's go."

I trample my way through the rest of the woods, careful not to trip and fall. Relief washes over me when we make it to the bottom. There's no way in hell we can go back to Joey's house. The best thing to do is to get in the river and ride this thing out.

A car engine vibrates among the trees.

"We've got to jump and I mean now!" I yell.

A cool breeze whips through me before my feet hits the water. The river engulfs all around me. I hold my breath and swim like a fish in the sea. The worst thing that could happen is this car finding the three of us in the water.

A minute passes by before I come up for air. The car's not anywhere to be seen. I'm sure it will be coming back.

Heather and Brooke both swim over to me. "What are we going to do?" Heather's teeth chatters when she speaks.

This water cuts through the core of my body like a cold winter day. To say this water is fucking cold is an understatement. I could care less about that. Being in this water is what's going to keep us safe. "We're going to stay in this water and get the fuck away from here," I say.

I'm not sure where we'll come out at. Either way it will be safer than being here.

I CAN'T BELIEVE any of this. We could've prevented this from happening. It's nobody's fault but my own for being so stupid. Brooke, Heather, and Sunny all have got to be alive. If they're not I'll be on the verge of insanity.

I pace around the parking lot. I'm about to come undone. "We've got to get back to the farm. I don't give a fuck how many people are there."

Wyatt nods. "Get in the fucking vehicle we're going."

My heart batters out of my chest as I think about the three of them. I hope those sick fuck's didn't do anything to them. They're all people who matter to me and don't deserve bad shit handed to them.

Ava wraps her fingers through mine. "Just breathe and relax. We're going back to get them."

I push her fingers away with my hand and step into the car. "You don't need to sugar coat anything. I'm fully prepared for the worst."

Ava sits on the other side of the car away from me. I'm not worried about her right now. I can't lose the family I once had. Maybe this with Ava wasn't such a good idea after all.

"Dad, what's going on?" Landon's voice is urgent.

"There's more people at the farm than what we originally thought." It hurts saying those words.

Wyatt starts the engine and I'm on the verge of going insane. Everything just seems like a complete blur passing me by.

I'm unable to say anything for everything eating away at my soul. I wasn't the nicest to Brooke or Heather at the farm. An asshole is what I was and it's not something I'll ever be proud of.

I refused to give Heather a second chance and it doesn't bother me. She's still a friend even though she'll never be my lover again. The first woman I've ever loved is her. Even if it wasn't the right kind of love.

Brooke will always be the closest thing I'll ever come close to having as a daughter. I regret not letting her search for Matt. She should've been able to go out there and try to find him. I strongly believe she would have grown accustomed to the ways of the world. After all she's young.

Sunny has been through a world of hurt because of so much loss. I refuse to believe he's gone out of this world a broken man. It doesn't settle right with me and makes my skin crawl.

They've all got to be alive. I need them here with me. God, don't tell me we're too late.

CHAPTER 37
SUNNY

I GET up out of the water and take a deep breath. There's overgrown brush all around us. My eye catches on a bench just a couple of yards away. It's then that it hits me. We're down by the walking track.

Heather comes up out of the water her teeth chattering. "What are we going to do next?"

"We're going to get out of here and start walking towards the road," I say.

We should be able to find a car and get out of here before nightfall. It's not going to be easy. Our best chances of survival are getting away from this area. I'm not sure where we'll go but don't care about that right now.

Brooke limps when she steps out of the water. "How far are we walking?" Her voice cracks.

I sure as hell hate that she's in pain.

I shrug. "There should be a house close by with a car."

A sports utility vehicle comes driving our way. There's a dent in the front and it's the same one Wyatt was driving earlier. I've got to let them know we're here and not at the farm. They can't go back there it's like a death sentence waiting to happen.

I run as fast as I can up the road and wave my hands in

front of me. The vehicle comes to a stop and Wyatt rolls down his window. "Heather and Brooke are down by the walking track."

I hop into the SUV and slide into the middle seat by myself. It feels good to be able to catch my breath. "The farm's destroyed. There's too many of those psychos around."

"I'm just happy you're all alive," Joey replies.

Wyatt drives down to get Brooke and Heather. The two of them get in the SUV beside me.

Now that the farm is destroyed here comes the hard part. I just hope we're all strong enough to survive and live in this world. Cause if we're not we'll be knocking on death's door.

Look for the Devil's Refuge on December 3, 2022.